Vanilla Fudge

Lizzie looked at the clean, milk-white fur of the puppy, the patches of caramel. There were several freckles on its nose too.

Lizzie was a child used to getting her own way.

"It's the one I want," she said firmly.

Mrs Doyle looked taken aback.

"No, I had really decided…"

"I don't mind paying a bit more," Mr Aubrey said. "How much do you want?"

Lizzie wasn't listening. She left them to it; she knew her dad would win. She was holding her very own puppy.

"Hello puppy," she whispered. And the puppy looked up at her, and sniffed her curiously.

Other Hippo Animal Stories:

Thunderfoot
Deborah van der Beek

A Foxcub Named Freedom
Brenda Jobling

Midnight Dancer
Midnight Dancer: To Catch a Thief
Midnight Dancer: Running Free
Midnight Dancer: Fireraisers
Elizabeth Lindsay

Animal Rescue
Bette Paul

Vanilla Fudge

Deborah van der Beek

Scholastic Children's Books,
Commonwealth House, 1-19 New Oxford Street,
London, WC1A 1NU, UK
a division of Scholastic Publications Ltd
London ~ New York ~ Toronto ~ Sydney ~ Auckland

First published by Scholastic Ltd, 1996

ISBN: 0 590 13497 3

Typeset by TW Typesetting, Midsomer Norton, Avon

Printed by Cox & Wyman, Reading, Berks

10 9 8 7 6 5 4

The right of Deborah van der Beek to be identified as the author of
this work has been asserted by her in accordance with the Copyright,
Designs and Patents Act, 1988.

For Margaret Luttrell, who has helped so many children enjoy so many books

Chapter 1

Even though everything hurt so much she could hardly think, Lizzie knew what to answer:

"A puppy."

Mr and Mrs Aubrey leaned towards their daughter, scarcely daring to believe she had spoken – it had been so long; almost two days they had waited. It was hot in the hospital and a wisp of hair stuck to her cheek with sweat; Mrs Aubrey reached out and brushed it gently away. For all those long hours the doctors and nurses had rushed back and forth, flipping the pale, loose body to check this, change that.

They had just sat by Lizzie's side, waiting, hoping.

"Lizzie?" Mr Aubrey said, for Lizzie's eyes had closed again. "Just get better. When you're better, if that's what you really want, you shall have a puppy."

Lizzie didn't open her eyes or answer; it was too much effort. She just smiled. A big smile that lit up her fat, doughy face, and made it look, for a moment, almost pretty.

Mrs Aubrey had taken Lizzie's hand. Now she looked up at her husband. "A puppy? Oh Jack, do you really think...?" She stopped. It was not the time to worry about whether they wanted a puppy or not: the only important thing now was that Lizzie should get well.

"She's asleep," Mr Aubrey said. "And she looks really peaceful. Don't you think that's a good sign?"

"It's wonderful," said Mrs Aubrey with feeling. "Really wonderful."

As Lizzie got better, Mrs Aubrey spoke again about the promise her husband had made.

"I do think you were unwise," she said.

"Oh, dear. I suppose you're right." Mr Aubrey looked guilty. "A cat would be less trouble, but you're both allergic. At least we know she isn't allergic to dogs."

"A dog," said Mrs Aubrey, "is a big responsibility. Is Lizzie ready for that yet?"

Mr Aubrey thought of the expensive toys flung in wild abandon round Lizzie's room. He remembered nights when Bella the aupair was off duty: the nasty crunching sounds underfoot when he tried to find a way through to kiss Lizzie good night.

"Then there's the rest of it," Mrs Aubrey carried on. "I mean we're not a doggy sort of family, are we? Can you imagine a dog in our house? Muddy paws, hairs everywhere. Smells." She shuddered.

"Well..." Mr Aubrey looked uncomfortable. "She's very muzzy with all those drugs. Perhaps she'll forget it."

But Lizzie didn't forget.

She had really been very ill indeed. Lizzie was quite used to asthma attacks by now –

she'd had them all her life – but this was much the worst because it got mixed up with a bout of flu, making all sorts of other things pack up. Twice Lizzie had died – well, that was what one doctor said later – for her heart had actually stopped. Not that she remembered it, but it would be something to tell them at horrible old school.

Lizzie didn't much like school, and school didn't seem to like Lizzie. It was always at school she started her worst attacks. Because she had missed so much, she was behind in her work and she was too fat and asthmatic to join in the running-about games everyone played in the playground. So she just stood at the side with her nose in the air and pretended she didn't want to join in anyhow.

Sometimes Lizzie's mum invited children back, but it never worked. Lizzie liked showing off her expensive toys: she wanted people to see how good she was on a computer. But in her house, she wanted to be boss. She always had to win. And people didn't like that. Few came more than once.

* * *

When she was well enough, Lizzie got a dog book out of the hospital library. On every page there was a picture of a different breed of dog. How delicious to lie back in the pillows and dream! Sometimes it was an alert, intelligent German Shepherd Lizzie wanted, sometimes a faithful collie. Always it was a big dog though, and usually one that could be strong and fierce when she wanted it to.

Since she had been a bit better, Mr and Mrs Aubrey had gone back to work, taking it in turns to visit. Tonight, however, they both came in.

"Look!" Lizzie showed them the book. "I've almost decided – I was going to have a bull-terrier, but they're not as big as the ones I really like—"

Mr and Mrs Aubrey exchanged glances.

"Lizzie…" Mr Aubrey wasn't looking forward to this. "I think your mother and I need to have a little talk with you."

Something about his voice made Lizzie look at her parents sharply. Mrs Aubrey couldn't meet her daughter's eye. She let her husband do the talking.

Mr Aubrey tried to smile in a jolly sort of way. "Lizzie dear," he began. "Are you really sure it's a puppy you want? You see, your mother and I – well – that is, I'm sure there's something else you'd rather have instead?"

"Instead?"

"Now," Mr Aubrey made his voice sound excited. "There's a wonderful new computer system about to come on the market. I could get it for you – you'd be the very first to have it!" Mr Aubrey worked in computers. What he offered Lizzie would be very good indeed. But Lizzie was not impressed.

"What d'you mean? A computer instead of a puppy?" She looked horrified.

"It's really very special ... or it could be anything else."

"Lizzie darling," Mrs Aubrey said. "A puppy is a very big responsibility. It needs regular feeds, walks, training."

"I'll do that. I promise," Lizzie said.

"Lizzie, darling," Mrs Aubrey said again gently. "What we are saying is—"

Lizzie had turned white. Now she became very red.

"No!" she screamed. "No! No! No! I want a puppy! Not a stupid old computer. Just a puppy. I want one, I want one." Although she was far too old to do so Lizzie flung herself into her pillow and broke into wild, wheezy sobs.

Mr and Mrs Aubrey exchanged helpless glances.

Lizzie turned from the pillow; the face she showed was ugly as a gargoyle. "You promised," she whined. "You promised. You always say you've got to keep promises. If you keep your promise to give me a puppy, I'll keep mine to look after it. I promise."

So Lizzie was to get her puppy.

Chapter 2

Hannah breathed on the window pane, then drew a little dog on it with her finger. She turned back to her mother. "So we really might move from here?" Hannah's dark eyes looked larger than ever, she was so excited.

Ruth Wilder smiled. "I'm in no hurry. I want to wait for the right job." She turned a chair to face Hannah, and sat down in it. "We need to talk about all this properly. It's going to make big changes in our lives if I do this. You'll be changing school soon so it's a good time for me to move on. But my job shouldn't be far from wherever you go to school – I wouldn't even mind teaching at the same place."

Hannah screwed up her face thoughtfully. "I don't think I'd mind either. Unless everyone hated you; it'd be really embarrassing. Do you think you're popular?"

Hannah's mother laughed. "Drama teachers don't usually do too badly," she said. "When you were little, I could only work part time. Now you're bigger, having a full-time job will be better for both of us. It shouldn't be hard to get one – I know the school I teach at now has been very pleased with me. And – if you can manage on your own a bit – " she looked anxiously at Hannah – "I want to do a course called 'Music in Drama'. During the holidays."

"Oh." Hannah tried not to mind. But she did. Very much. "Of course I can manage," she said (though she spoke so her mother would know she really did mind).

Ruth Wilder ignored this. "We'll be able to afford all sorts of things we haven't been able to." Her eyes wandered round the cramped flat they had lived in since Hannah was born. "Like a bigger flat – one with a proper bed-room for you."

"And a garden?"

"And a garden … and then…"

"And then I can have a pet of my own!" Hannah forgot about minding. She plunked herself into the sagging sofa and lay with her feet hanging over the arm. When she spoke, it was from upside-down.

"I don't want a rabbit. A cat would be nice; but what I really, really want is a dog – a puppy, so we can see it grow up, and train it and all that. Oh, I can hardly wait," she said, hugging a cushion to her chest as though it were the puppy itself.

"You're squashing the poor thing," said her mother.

From then on, Hannah longingly scanned the "Pets" column in the local paper every Saturday: "Dalmatian pups, ready two weeks. Father pedigree prizewinner" or "Champion-bred German Shepherd puppies, to good homes only." Hannah was sure she must be a "good home" – or am I? she worried.

Ruth Wilder laughed. "I'm sure we'll be the very best, but," she said firmly, "don't get any ideas about a dog with a fancy pedigree – or a large one that costs a fortune to feed either. We've got to be sensible about this. We need something that's small and cheap to run."

"It's not a car!" cried Hannah, scandalized. But her mother was just teasing her.

"I've been looking at the small ads too," she said. "With all these changes coming to us I think it's about time we got ourselves a little car. I'll have much bigger choice of job then."

"A car!" Hannah was delighted. No more long waits at bus stops. No more struggling through the rain with heavy shopping. Wonderful!

"And Mum?" she said. "I don't mind about not having a pedigree dog – or a German Shepherd. I don't mind what I have – as long as it's a dog."

"Just wait," Hannah's mother said. "I haven't got the job yet."

Chapter 3

An Irish Wolfhound: that's it, Lizzie decided. She imagined the amazed gasps at school when she came in with such an enormous hairy creature. One word from Lizzie and the faithful hound would snarl at anyone she chose... Only Lizzie it would love and protect to the ends of the earth. Just let them refuse to be impressed by an Irish Wolfhound – even as a puppy it would be huge! Mrs Aubrey (as Lizzie knew she would) almost had a fit at the idea.

But it was Lizzie's father who put his finger on the truth of the matter. "You've just been ill," he said firmly. "A big dog like that needs an enormous amount of exercise – and some one very experienced to train it."

Lizzie knew he was right, which annoyed her; she sulked for the rest of the day. She wouldn't even cheer up when her father said he had found just the right puppy for her.

"But I don't want a cocker spaniel," she said sourly. "I want an Irish Wolfhound."

"These ones are ready on Saturday; they'll be seven weeks old then. And pedigree – well, a queen would be proud to have as good."

"Saturday! But it's Wednesday now…" An Irish Wolfhound in the misty future was one thing. A real live puppy, already born and waiting for her was quite another… Only three more days and she could actually be holding her very own puppy. What a pity it was just a cocker spaniel…

"Only old ladies have cocker spaniels," she said. "I'll think about it. I might."

But the following day Lizzie rushed out of school in a panic. "If I do decide to have it, we haven't got anything ready." So she and Bella the au-pair took a taxi to the department store in town. Bella waited while Lizzie gathered a pile of things the saleswoman told her were absolutely essential to the happiness of her (possible) puppy-to-be.

"A big dog is it – or just a little one?"

That "just" decided Lizzie: she'd go along on Saturday just to see, but she thought she'd wait for what she really wanted. Her parents always gave in to her in the end.

"Well, it might be an Irish Wolfhound."

"An Irish Wolfhound! Goodness me! You'll need our very largest! Would Madam be wanting our regular model, or our DeLuxe Plus in naturally finished Somerset caning with double-tog duvet-style blanket? It's specially designed with comfort in mind."

"The DeLuxe," said Lizzie without hesitation.

Bella and she could barely get in the taxi back home. Mr Aubrey gulped when he saw the bill, but said nothing: he was glad to see Lizzie so excited about something. It meant she was getting well.

Chapter 4

At the kennels on Saturday Lizzie put on a cold, blank expression: she wasn't going to be pushed into anything against her will.

Mrs Doyle the breeder had a squidgy face like a putty rubber. Her mouth was painted orange and every time she moved a cloud of face powder rose in the air: her yellow cardigan was quite pink over the shoulders, making her look (Lizzie thought) like a sunset.

She gave Lizzie a sharp look. Was this sourfaced young girl going to love and care for a puppy as she ought? Mrs Doyle liked to feel she was careful about the homes she let her dogs go to.

Mr Aubrey wrinkled up his nose. The place smelt terrible; it was only what any large group of dogs smell like, but Mr Aubrey was horrified. Would their house smell like this? His wife would hate it.

Lizzie looked at the pens full of spaniels of all colours and sizes. They were all leaping up and barking excitedly.

"The babies are inside," Mrs Doyle said. "I always keep my boys and girls in the kitchen while they are small. I expect there's a bit of a mess... Ooh! You naughty little things."

A bit! Mr Aubrey turned quite pale. Although the floor had only just been wiped, already several puddles had appeared. Trails of a rather smelly dog food led from a bowl and all over the kitchen. But Lizzie let out a gasp of delight. Six plump puppies tumbled and played about their black-and-white mother, pulling at her ears and nuzzling her for milk.

Mrs Doyle sent the mother outside while they looked at the puppies. "Not that she'd

snap at you – none of my dogs are allowed to – it's just that she'd get in the way. She'd prefer it if nobody touched her puppies at all." The black-and-white bitch went off with great reluctance, looking back over her shoulder and walking very slowly.

"Out, Sunshine, shoo!" scolded Mrs Doyle.

Lizzie knelt down to see the puppies better. They had long, silky ears and huge floppy paws. You could see exactly what they were thinking by the way their faces wrinkled. She was beginning to think she might not mind a spaniel after all (though she wasn't going to let anyone else know just yet).

"The two little black boys are taken … and I think I'm keeping the orange-and-white girl," Mrs Doyle said.

"That leaves the goldy one and two black-and-white." Lizzie frowned. She looked at each of them in turn. The golden one snuffled and looked at her with its head on one side. Then it squealed, because one of the others had attacked its tail with sharp teeth. Mrs Doyle laughed, sending pink powder flying

round the kitchen. She picked the attacker up and handed it to Lizzie. The puppy whined. It felt all warm and wobbly in her hands.

"This is the one you're keeping," Lizzie said. "Why this one?"

"It's the best," Mrs Doyle said. "Good personality. Good clean lines. She'll be a smasher in the show ring, that one."

Lizzie looked at the clean, milk-white fur of the puppy, the patches of caramel. There were several freckles on its nose too. Poor little thing. Was it going to have to spend its life being shampooed and hanging around dog shows?

Lizzie was a child used to getting her own way.

"It's the one I want," she said firmly.

Mrs Doyle looked taken aback.

"No, I had really decided..."

"I don't mind paying a bit more," Mr Aubrey said. "How much do you want?"

Mrs Doyle decided she had been right about the girl. And children were like puppies. It didn't do to spoil them.

Mr Aubrey looked at his daughter. Lizzie was clutching the puppy as if her life depended on it. Maybe it did. And then if they didn't get this one... He thought about the Irish Wolfhound and shuddered.

"I really—" Mrs Doyle began again.

"Double," said Mr Aubrey. "I'll pay double."

Lizzie wasn't listening. She left them to it; she knew her dad would win. She was holding her very own puppy.

"Hello puppy," she whispered. And the

puppy looked up at her, and sniffed her curiously.

Chapter 5

Lizzie held the puppy in her lap all the way home. It hunched silently into her arms, every now and then licking her hand with a timid, pink tongue.

Safe in the glove compartment of the car were the precious papers saying Lizzie was now the owner of "Spaniel (Cocker) Registration No. U1623004U02. Name: Bathsheba Joyous Sunrise of Chingford."

"Do I have to call her all that?" Lizzie had asked Mrs Doyle uneasily.

"Oh, no. That's just her Kennel Club name – what you would call her if you put her into a show. You saw her mother – Sunshine? Her real name is just as long, and her father we just call Bob, though his name is … now let me think … 'Soul of Solomon Happy Rascal the Seventeenth'."

Lizzie had heaved a sigh of relief.

Even Mrs Aubrey let out a cry of delight when she saw the puppy, and Bella wanted to hold her immediately.

"Is dear!" Bella cried. "So, so sweeeet."

Lizzie beamed with pride. "I think she's sweet too – and I've already decided what I'm calling her. Mum and Bella – this is Fudge."

Fudge sat where Lizzie had put her. At first she seemed too scared to make a noise, or even look about her.

"Is she hungry?" asked Mrs Aubrey.

"Mrs Doyle said she might not eat much at first. She gave me some special puppy food you mix with milk. I've got to give her that four times a day."

"Four times! I thought you only fed dogs once a day."

"She's only got a little stomach," Mr

Aubrey pointed out. "I expect she needs it filled little and often."

"Yes," Lizzie smiled. "And can we get some more of this food? Mrs Doyle said we should stick to it for a while as anything else might upset her tummy."

Lizzie kept Fudge with her all that first day. She could hardly bear to put her down, and carried her with her everywhere.

Fudge didn't seem to mind; she was still a bit nervous of her new home. She ate a bit, explored a bit and fell asleep in Lizzie's lap. After every meal, and every time she woke, Lizzie carried her into the garden for house-training. It was just as Mrs Doyle had said. If you watched carefully you could tell just when she needed to go: first she would start sniffing about, then she would turn in circles, then she did a dropping. It's all going so well, Lizzie thought happily. This isn't going to be hard at all.

At bedtime she spread newspapers all over the floor – you can't expect a puppy to last all

night without a pee. Then she put Fudge in her basket and patted her good night.

The basket looked ridiculously large. Fudge watched Lizzie with large brown eyes, and then, to Lizzie's horror, she began to tremble all over.

"Are you cold?" Lizzie tucked the Super-Soft duvet-style blanket round her, but Fudge trembled even more. What should she do? There was no one about – both Bella and her mother were out, and anyway they probably wouldn't be much use. Mr Aubrey

was in his study, but he had asked not to be
disturbed except in an emergency. Was this
an emergency? Lizzie decided that it was.
However, the moment she left the room, the
puppy began to cry. There was no other word
for it; it sounded just like crying. And it was
all the more startling because up until then,
she hadn't made a sound.

"*Eeeehooo–oooeee–eee–eee...*"

Panic-stricken, Lizzie ran back into the
room and picked Fudge up. The noise
stopped immediately. The puppy snuggled

in, tail wagging. Lizzie put her down and tried to go again, this time creeping away quietly. But the puppy wouldn't have it: the second Lizzie began to close the door, the noise began and she had to come back.

Lizzie tried hard to understand. If only Fudge could talk – but the puppy remained obstinately silent. It just looked sadder and sadder.

Lizzie had never thought much about anyone's troubles but her own; this was quite new to her. She thought of the kitchen at Mrs Doyle's, the six tumbling puppies, and the comforting warmth of the mother dog. Could Fudge be homesick? Suddenly Lizzie had a brainwave: a hot-water bottle. The puppy could snuggle up to that as if it were another dog. It would be warm and comforting.

Lizzie hadn't heated water up before. Somehow, if you were ill a lot, people did things for you. She worked out how to put the kettle on, and after some searching, found a hot-water bottle with a thick woolly cover.

Fudge watched her all the time. Lizzie

wasn't used to animals, and she felt a bit silly talking to something that couldn't understand. But the way Fudge's ears moved forward to listen made her carry on.

"Fudge? I'm just making sure the bottle isn't too hot… Then I'll give it to you. I'm calling you Fudge because Fudge is my best kind of sweet. Do you like the name Fudge?"

But the puppy yawned, and when Lizzie tucked the bottle in under her blanket, she wriggled up and fell fast asleep.

Lizzie sat and watched the rising and falling of the plump body, pink on its belly where the fur was thinner, and the golden brown silky ears. She felt a warm glow of pride at having got something right.

When her dad came in to kiss her good night Lizzie hugged him so tight his stubbly chin left marks on her cheek.

"Thankyou thankyou thankyou thank you!" she said. "I know I'm really going to like having Fudge – looking after her, training her and everything."

In the dark, Mr Aubrey smiled. It was good to see her so happy.

"You may have to do a lot more of it than I expected," he said. "I have to go away soon — to Germany."

"Oh, yes?" Lizzie was suddenly gloomy: she hated it when her dad went away for long.

"It's for a customer of mine whose factory is there. He wants me to design some new computer parts for him specially. It will be a very big order." Mr Aubrey frowned. "You know we used to go to Wales a lot for holidays?"

"Uncle Ralph's cottage," Lizzie said.

"Do you remember that strange place nearby — the one with all the high fences round it?"

"Mr Barbed Wire's?"

"Yes, that's what we called it. That's him. My new client."

"No!" Lizzie's eyes widened. How could she forget Mr Barbed Wire? They had all been so curious about this odd, secretive man, whom nobody had seen. No one even knew his name. He had bought the house next to Uncle Ralph's cottage and put up high fences all round – even round quite ordinary-looking fields. And not only was the fence high, but there were curved bits at the top making it impossible to climb over.

"Who is he then? What's he called? What's he like?"

Mr Aubrey thought. "He's called Smith, and he seems quite ordinary to me; brown hair, smallish, thinnish. I've heard he can be difficult. That's all."

Lizzie was disappointed. "But he must be... I mean, why all the barbed wire?" A sudden thought struck her. "Hey, can we go there when you get back? The cottage, I mean? Fudge would love it."

Mr Aubrey stood up to go.

"It's a good idea," he said. "Sleep well."

The following morning, Bella shook Lizzie awake. It was still dark; it must be very early.

"Your leetle dog."

"Fudge."

"Fug. Is sad. Is crying. And mess! Is – "
The face Bella made would be understood in
any language. "Ai-yeugh!"

"Oh, dear."

The noise was terrible. It sort of twisted
your heart. Lizzie couldn't understand why
she hadn't been woken up by it. "*Eeeeeoooo-
ooh* (sigh) *Oooooohoohoohoo* (heavy sigh)..."
and on and on. She pulled a dressing-gown
round her and ran downstairs.

From that moment Lizzie realized what hard
work a puppy was. And it was she, Lizzie,
who had to do it all.

Mr and Mrs Aubrey had taken time off
when Lizzie was ill; now they were busy
catching up. And Bella squealed "I weel fai-
eent, I weel fai-eent!" when she discovered a
(very small) dropping in her bedroom.

House-training a puppy isn't easy. You
think they've got it at last and – whoops! –
there's another.

"Oh, no!" cried Mrs Aubrey, feeling something squishy under her foot again. Mrs

Aubrey was rather bad-tempered these days. Maybe it was the extra work, but she kept getting headaches.

"Oh, Lizzie! Clear it up, will you?" she said crossly. "I must get myself an aspirin."

Lizzie looked guilty; she had known the dropping was there, but had hoped someone else would see to it.

Having Fudge was the most marvellous thing that had ever happened to Lizzie. Clearing Fudge's mess was not.

Chapter 6

Sometimes Hannah opened a paper and read about the most senseless cruelty to animals. Who were these people? she wondered. Why did they do such disgusting things? Most of all, what would she do if she saw it happening? Would she be brave or know what to do?

"So. Two pounds of coxes — small ones, 'cause they're cheaper — some tomatoes, a lettuce, and go and pay the butcher's bill," Hannah repeated.

Hannah's mother frowned. "I don't like giving you so much. Twenty pounds is a lot of money."

"Don't worry," Hannah said. "Look, I'm zipping it into my inside pocket. I can't possibly lose it. And I'll put the change in my purse."

Hannah walked along with her hands in her pockets, dreamily staring at the ground and thinking of nothing in particular. If she hadn't walked into someone, she probably would not even have noticed. She bumped into the old lady, because the old lady was standing in the middle of the pavement staring at three boys over the road. They weren't very old, but they looked quite tough and determined, and they were dragging a small animal behind them. It was so wet and caked with mud that it was several moments before Hannah realized that it was a dog – a puppy. Like the old lady, she froze. The boys had the puppy on a long piece of string, and they were pulling it through puddles, and laughing because it kept losing its balance. It wasn't making much protest, because every time it was jerked forward, the string round its neck got tighter and tighter.

Hannah realized that the old lady had moved on, trotting away as fast as she could. Hannah was on her own.

"What can I do? I should cross the road and stop them. I should. I must." But Hannah wasn't brave. And although the boys were about her own age, they were much tougher and there were three of them.

Just then, the puppy looked at her – and as it did so, the largest of the boys gave it a kick that sent it flying to the end of the string. Hannah felt her knees give way, but saved herself just in time, and crossed the road. Frantically scrabbling to open her jacket, she held something out to them. She was so frightened she couldn't speak.

The smallest boy stepped forward to look. His eyes widened. "Twenty pound!" He looked at the older one.

For a moment, Hannah thought they were just going to snatch the money and run, but they must have been tired of lugging an animal about. Two seconds later, she watched as the boys ran off into the distance, and she was left holding a piece of string with the puppy on the end of it. Suddenly her head began to swim. She sat down on the pavement with the puppy in her lap, and, tearing at the string round its neck with fierce hands, burst into tears.

The puppy was surprisingly heavy to carry such a long way, and by the time she got home, Hannah's arms ached terribly.

"Mum?"

Hearing something odd in her voice, Ruth Wilder came quickly. Hannah held the puppy out so that her mother could see. "Mum…" She began to cry again. "Mum… I spent the twenty pounds. I'm sorry. I – I just had to." Tears were running down her face so fast now that she couldn't wipe them away and it was some time before her mother could find out what had happened.

"Oh, Mum, it was so horrible. How could they?" Hannah said it over and over again.

Ruth Wilder put an arm round her. "I don't know. There are just some things we never understand. I think you were very brave."

"But that's just it! I wasn't. I was pathetic. I just stood there – for ages. I let him *kick* it."

All this time, the puppy had been lying quietly in her arms. Now it reached up and licked her face.

"There you are," said her mother. "The puppy says it doesn't mind. It's safe now. And it doesn't matter about the money. It's only money."

"But it doesn't grow on trees," Hannah said anxiously, and her mother laughed.

"No. But we'll make do. Lots of lentils and beans?"

"Yuck!" said Hannah, beginning to smile. She pulled the animal towards her and buried her nose in its muddy fur. "Mum, he's cold. He's shivering."

"It's a 'she', I think," said her mother. "You hold on to her while I get some hot water ready – we can use that old baby bath."

Hannah held the puppy while her mother rubbed it gently all over. At first it just sat in frozen terror, but after a bit it began to look around in an interested sort of way. Dirt and grime floated off.

They took her out and towelled her dry; very carefully in case there were any bruises. Then they put her in a cardboard box with an old blanket in it and set it by the fire. She fell fast asleep immediately.

"Poor thing; the shock must have exhausted her. She seems fine, but we'll take her in to a vet tomorrow, just in case," Ruth Wilder said. She looked at the puppy with her head on one side. "I don't know what you think, but I'd say she was a spaniel of some kind. A cocker perhaps. She's a lovely colour."

"Like vanilla ice-cream with toffee in it," agreed Hannah. "Mmmm!"

"Call her that then," said her mother. "Vanilla."

"Mum?" Hannah looked at her mother anxiously. "Are we going to keep her? I mean we weren't supposed to get a puppy just yet."

"Keep her? I don't think I could bear to have any other now. Anyway, you bought her."

"So – this is it; it's really happened."

Hannah's smile was enormous. She looked at the puppy's round white tummy.

"Vanilla… I think that's fair," Hannah said. "I chose her, so you choose the name. Anyway, I like it."

So Vanilla it was.

"You're shivering!" said Ruth Wilder suddenly. She frowned at her daughter. "You've had a shock too – dealing with those hooligans. Right. A hot bath, and off to bed with you for the rest of the day."

"Me?"

"Yes, you." Hannah hadn't noticed how wet and dirty her clothes were. Now she had begun to feel cold too. She tried to hide the chattering of her teeth because she couldn't bear to leave the sleeping puppy. She could still hardly believe it was true.

"But—"

"Off!" Hannah had no option but to obey.

Chapter 7

The blue BMW drew smoothly away from the restaurant.

Lizzie had been a bit worried about leaving Fudge alone in the house, for Bella was out too. She hoped there wouldn't be any puddles or dog messes; her parents made such a fuss about them. Still, it had been a nice meal – a sort of goodbye celebration for her parents: Mrs Aubrey had decided to go with Lizzie's father to Germany. Lizzie was to be left in the charge of Bella. She wasn't too happy about the idea.

"Why do you have to go for so long? And why both of you? And why so far?"

"I thought your mother could do with a

holiday — all these headaches she's been having. There's a very nice Health Farm in the mountains nearby. She can relax there and get better while I work."

"Hmmm…" Lizzie didn't sound convinced. Then she brightened. "You'll be able to find out all about Mr Barbed Wire too, Mum. I don't mind being left too much really – not now I've got Fudge."

Mrs Aubrey smiled affectionately at her daughter: Fudge came into everything these days. It really seemed to have done Lizzie the world of good; not only was she a lot easier to get on with, but she looked better – happier. What a pity these headaches stopped her from enjoying it all… Never mind, they were sure to go as soon as she had a holiday.

"Good old Fudge. And don't you worry – I'll find out all I can about Mr Barbed Wire – I'm as curious as you."

Just then the BMW slowed down and they swung into the drive.

"Oh-oh," said Mr Aubrey suddenly. "Something's wrong."

"What do you mean?" Mrs Aubrey said.

"We've had visitors." He parked the car and pointed to a small window at the corner of the house. A pane had been smashed and the window was hanging open. Now they looked closer they could see muddy footmarks streaked down the walls where the intruder or intruders had climbed in.

"I hope they haven't done too much damage." Mr Aubrey spoke grimly. He fumbled with his keys in his anxiety.

It was terrible. For several moments they just stood and gaped: the burglars hadn't stuck to taking things, but had smashed and spoiled everything they could. Drawers were pulled out, the contents spilled everywhere. Bits of china lay all over the floor and bottles had been deliberately broken and trodden into the carpet.

"I'll get on to the police," said Mrs Aubrey. She spoke into a silence. A complete and utter deadness. No excited whine, no bouncing and scuffling. No Fudge.

Chapter 8

Hannah held Vanilla as directed. It wasn't easy, as the table was slippery, and her paws scudded in all directions. She was trembling like a leaf.

The vet gave her a friendly rub behind the ears. "Nice little thing, aren't you?" he said.

Vanilla still trembled, but her tail began to wag a bit and she looked much less frightened. He felt her all over, checking every part. "A rescue job, was she?"

Hannah nodded, telling him how she had found the puppy.

"A good thing you got to her in time. I really don't understand people like that."

"Is she all right?" Hannah asked.

"She'll be fine. There's a bit of bruising here and there, especially round her neck, here – " he parted the fur to show a nasty ring of swollen blue, with the soft skin broken in a number of places – "and here – but it's nothing serious. I'm putting some antiseptic ointment on, and I'll give her an antibiotic jab just to be on the safe side."

Hannah turned away when the needle went in, but Vanilla didn't even notice.

"In fact she's remarkably healthy for a pup with such a bad start: well fed, no fleas – though you ought to worm her, just in case," the vet said. "I'd guess she's about twelve or thirteen weeks old, and yes, a cocker spaniel. She seems a friendly soul – I'd say you'd got quite a bargain."

He told Hannah to keep Vanilla inside for a few days, and to be very gentle and quiet with her.

This turned out to be hard. Though timid at first, Vanilla quickly became very lively indeed. She raced about the sitting room chasing an old teddy bear Hannah threw and turning mad somersaults where her claws skidded from the rug on to lino. Vanilla looked a bit surprised, but it didn't seem to bother her, for off she raced a moment later to do exactly the same thing on the other side of the room. Hannah laughed out loud to see the expression of wrinkled pride as she sat with the teddy grasped firmly in her jaws.

"Hmmm." Hannah's mother surveyed the battle-torn sitting room a few days later: a puppy certainly didn't help when it came to keeping the place looking tidy. And – she drew her breath in sharply. Oh, no! She stooped to pick up an exercise-book. "Jessica Braith— (splodge). Form— (splodge)." The edges of the blue exercise-book were a mass of tiny punched tooth-holes. How would she explain to Jessica Braithwaite that her precious play had been chewed by a puppy? And this was just a wee thing of thirteen weeks! How much worse would the damage be in six months' time? Ruth Wilder decided then and there that she would find the new job and move as soon as possible. Now she said: "Right. Out, you two – that puppy is ready for a walk in the park. Now."

Hannah needed no second bidding. She flew to the drawer where she had put the soft blue puppy collar. They bounded out together.

Vanilla was overjoyed to be let free. She zoomed about with her ears flapping like propellers; but she always kept her eye on Hannah, and never went far away.

After that, Hannah took her out all the time. Every day that passed, Vanilla grew bigger and stronger. She was beginning to lose her wobbly baby looks and become leggy. The fluffy puppy fur was going, and Hannah could see the beginnings of "feather" along her tummy and the backs of her legs: all spaniels have this lovely, silky feather. As with other gun-dogs, bred for an outdoor life, thick fur helps keep them warm, and the feathering acts as a sort of "run-off" when they get wet.

Hannah loved coming home from school

now. On the days when her mother worked she didn't come into an empty house. Now, the moment her key turned in the lock she would hear a scuffle of paw-nails and opened the door to a small excited body, flinging itself at her. Vanilla would leap up and down, squeaking with happiness, tail wagging as fast as it could go.

It is nice to be loved.

Hannah had always been good at drawing – very good. Now in the evenings, when she and

the puppy were tired after a long walk, she
drew her. Drawing dogs before, there were
some bits she could never get right. Now she
could draw from life. She filled sketch-book
after sketch-book with pictures of Vanilla –
asleep, running, jumping, sitting. She drew
Vanilla the way she looked when she thought
she was going to get fed, and Vanilla sad
(when it wasn't time yet). She even drew
Vanilla yawning. Mrs Currey, her art teacher
at school, was amazed.

"Hannah, these are really very special.

Look, I've just been sent details of a competition between all schools in the county. Would you mind if I put one in? You are certainly the best hope from our school."

Hannah blushed and nodded: she had always known she wanted to be an artist, but she had rather supposed it would all happen when she left school. Now, here was Mrs Currey saying she was their "best hope".

"Wow!" Hannah said. "Is that really the prize? I wouldn't mind fifty pounds to spend on books and art materials! And – " as a thought occurred to her – "I could pay Mum back the twenty pounds for Vanilla."

She and Mrs Currey went through the drawings, and finally agreed on one of Vanilla when she saw a cat for the first time. You could see all the tenseness of her muscles; she was dying to chase it but a bit scared. Her ears were pricked forward, and Hannah had drawn the cat, not bothered at all, just disappearing round a corner.

"It's a bit … well, unfinished–looking," Hannah said. "I mean it was only a sketch."

"It's full of life," said Mrs Currey. "But if you like, put in a bit of colour – not much, you don't want to spoil it."

So Hannah very carefully put in some grass, and painted in Vanilla's markings – the speckles on her nose, the patches on her head and body.

"Now forget about it," Mrs Currey advised. "Then we won't be disappointed if nothing happens."

So Hannah did – for the moment.

Chapter 9

The night Fudge disappeared Lizzie felt as if she had lost a part of herself, as if an arm or leg had been chopped off. She didn't know what to do with herself.

While the police took down details in the house, Lizzie searched the dark garden, calling and calling. Sometimes she turned off the torch and just stood, listening. Suppose Fudge was hiding somewhere, frightened by all the noise? With her heart in her mouth she went outside in the street and searched up and down, hoping she wouldn't find the thing she feared most of all: a small brown-and-white body lying in the gutter.

It was over an hour before her father found her. He was furious. "Lizzie! Why didn't you tell us where you were going? We've been frantic ... losing you on top of everything else."

Lizzie spoke fiercely. "It's Fudge who's lost, not me. I'm not coming in till I find her!"

"It's late, Lizzie. You won't find her now." Even as he spoke, the torch faltered, then faded out. In the sudden darkness, Lizzie sniffed. Mr Aubrey put his arm round her. He could feel the sobs shaking her.

"Come in to bed," he said more gently. "I expect she'll turn up in the morning. She won't have gone far."

But Fudge didn't turn up.

Lizzie had never felt more lonely or miserable in her life. Although her mum stayed on an extra couple of days to sort things out, soon she was gone too. Lizzie was left alone with Bella.

Bella tried to be sympathetic, but Lizzie was beyond cheering.

"Have you ringed the police again?" Bella asked.

"Oh, could you, Bella?" Lizzie asked.

Bella looked alarmed. "No ... my English ... you must do so."

"Me?" Lizzie hadn't thought of that. It seemed the sort of thing grown-ups did for you. "I ... I suppose I could."

But the police weren't much help. "... only a dog – it could be anywhere. We've got a good chance of finding the video – your dad marked it, you see."

"I don't care about the video. I want Fudge."

"Fudge? Is that the little dog's name? I expect it'll turn up. It probably just ran off somewhere. Well, at least we've had no reports of dogs being run over. Have you tried the Dog's Home? We're very busy, you know."

So Lizzie tried the Dog's Home. No luck.

Lizzie tried everything she could think of. If her parents had been around, they would have done it all for her. Now she had to think for herself. She wrote out notices and put them up everywhere she thought people would see them. She did them in her best handwriting, and made sure each one was clear, and gave her name and telephone number. She didn't think Fudge could have got far; she wasn't very strong yet.

Every time the doorbell rang, Lizzie raced to see who it was. Every time the phone went, her heart started to beat faster. Was it an answer to one of her notices?

But it was only the postman at the door, only another phone call for Bella. Sometimes there were letters or postcards from Mr or Mrs Aubrey. These said things like "Having a wonderful time – wish you were with us," or "Headaches completely gone – hope you've found Fudge." Lizzie felt lonelier than ever.

A whole week passed and nothing happened. Lizzie realized she was going to have to try harder. Now she took her notices further. She put some in shop windows, and one on the noticeboard of the big supermarket. Surely someone would see it? But still there was no news of Fudge.

Bella, who had disliked Lizzie almost since the day she arrived, began to admire her. Partly it was because Lizzie had been ill for so long she had had nothing to think about but herself. And her parents had spoiled and spoiled her. When Bella came, she was just beginning to get ill. Now she was better and she had Fudge to worry about too. Almost without noticing it, Bella began to like Lizzie. She started to help her. "I have idea," she said.

"An idea. I have an idea. I mean, I don't, I mean that's what you say."

Bella beamed. "Thank you. One moment please." She went and got her dictionary. "I think ... I think ... yes: 'reward'. Why don't you gives reward?"

"Bella! Of course – why didn't I think of it before?" Lizzie leapt up in delight. "And – " Lizzie flushed. She wasn't used to this sort of thing. "I mean, I know you don't like dogs much, so ... thanks."

"Fug is nice dog. Is 'er ... ploppings I don't like so well."

That evening, Bella and Lizzie made some

more notices. Bella was quite artistic and her lettering was much better than Lizzie's. Lizzie went over all the capital letters in red, to make them stand out. Now the notices read:

REWARD
Lost, Stolen or Strayed:
COCKER SPANIEL PUPPY
White with chestnut patches,
chestnut ears, few speckles on nose.
Answers to name of Fudge.

Lizzie got hold of a copy of the *Yellow Pages* and looked up all the newsagents. Then she phoned them up and asked if they had a noticeboard in their shop, and would they mind putting her notice up? Most said they would do it for nothing, so Lizzie posted a copy to each. There were twelve of them. Then she sat down and waited.

Chapter 10

"Hannah! That's wonderful – second prize! What's wrong?"

"Nothing," Hannah said.

"But why don't you want to win now?" Ruth Wilder asked. "I'm really looking forward to seeing it in the Central Library."

"I just don't want to, that's all. It's – it's not good enough."

"Don't be silly. Why, when it was first announced, you were so pleased." Hannah's mother was completely flummoxed. Hannah said nothing, but sat with Vanilla in her lap, hugging her close. Vanilla wriggled and pretended to bite Hannah.

"You're cross because you didn't come first? Is that it?" Now Ruth Wilder looked cross herself. "Because if you are…" Hannah hesitated, then looked at the ground and nodded.

"I'm ashamed of you, Hannah." Still cross, she added, "And that puppy needs a walk. You didn't take her on one this morning, did you?"

Hannah shook her head.

"Well, go on then. You aren't getting tired of her, are you?"

"Oh, no! It's just…" Hannah's face was dark and stiff. "I just don't feel like it, that's all."

"Well, the puppy does, so you'd better take her – I've got marking to do."

Vanilla knew she was going out. She started bouncing round Hannah's legs, leaping up to catch her attention. Slowly, without enthusiasm, Hannah got up and fetched the lead.

It was just the same the next day.

"Is there anything wrong, Hannah?"

"No, nothing." But Hannah's face was set at "stormy".

Ruth Wilder shrugged her shoulders helplessly: children could be such a puzzle sometimes.

Hannah chose a quiet road to the park, avoiding shops. Vanilla wasn't much good on a lead yet. She twisted this way and that and ran round Hannah in a circle so that they got in a hopeless tangle. Today she was worse than ever, and Hannah got cross. How could people not notice them if Vanilla behaved like that?

They went to a distant part of the park, where there were more trees and it was a bit wilder. Hannah wasn't really supposed to come here on her own as her mother warned her that there were sometimes "funny people" around. Vanilla flew off the lead, and hurtled about like a mad thing. She liked it much better here – there were humpy tussocks of grass to leap over and shrubs to hide in and leap out and surprise Hannah. Hannah wanted to practise calling the puppy to her, but Vanilla was in a disobedient mood.

Suddenly a man came towards them.

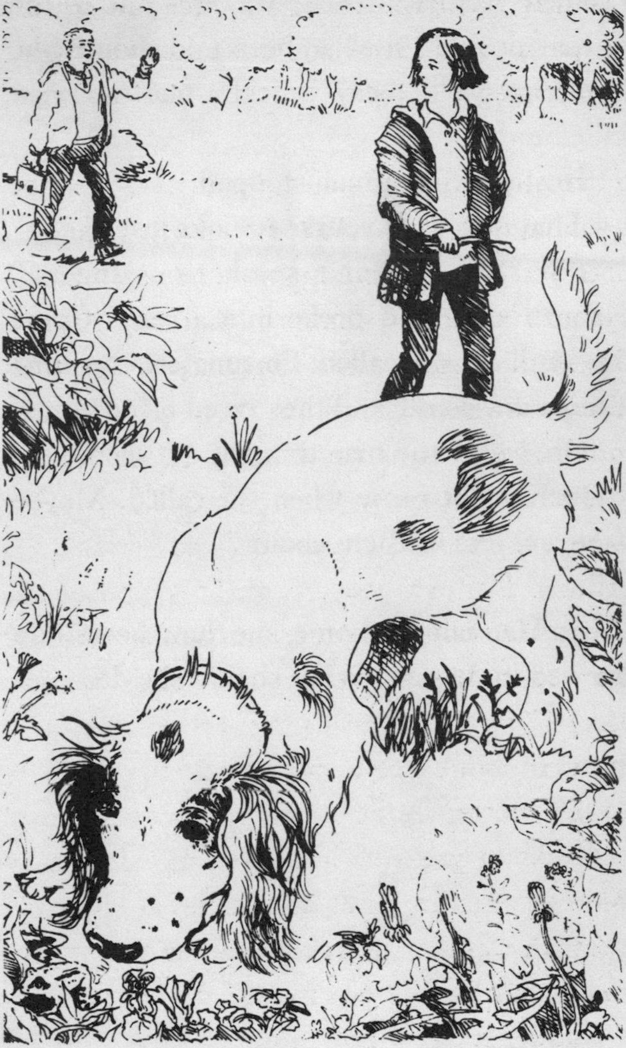

Hannah was frightened. Was this one of the "funny people" she had been told about? She began to walk away quickly, but the man called to her.

"Hey, you?" Hannah stopped.

"That dog. Is it yours? It looks just like—"

"I'm sorry, I don't speak to strangers," Hannah said, and broke into a run. "Come on, Vanilla," she called. Fortunately, this time Vanilla did come, and they raced off together.

"Oh, well," the man thought. "It seemed to know her – it came when she called. Maybe there are lots of them about."

When Hannah got home, she flung herself on her bed in despair. What should she do?

Chapter 11

"**D**on't get too excited," the woman on the phone said to Lizzie. "It might have been done from imagination – or it might just be another puppy the same colours."

"Yes, it might." Lizzie felt disappointed all over again. On the other hand, this was the first and only lead she had had so far. "Thank you very much," she said. "I will go and see it."

The Central Library was a huge building with wide steps in front as long as the building itself, and fat columns that held up a triangular bit on top. Bella wanted to take a photograph, so Lizzie posed for her. Lizzie hated being photographed, and she wanted to get on inside. She scowled gloomily.

And there it was! Lizzie stood in front of the picture and caught her breath. A peculiar feeling made the hairs on her neck and all down her back rise as if she had seen a ghost. Fudge! There was no doubt at all. Fudge – a little slimmer, a bit furrier, but definitely the same puppy: every marking, every speckle was right. It was a wonderful drawing. Lizzie looked at the picture next to it, which bore the sign "First Prize". It was a painting by a much younger child, a glorious splodge of colour. You couldn't really compare them.

She examined the drawing of Fudge more closely. There was no name attached, but in the corner, very small, were the initials "HW". How could she find out who "HW" was? Maybe the librarian would know?

But the man at the desk shook his head. "I'm not the one organizing the competition. The person who might know doesn't come in till Friday."

Friday! Ages away. Just then, a young

woman came up with a pile of books in her arms. "I know who it is," she said. "Well, sort of. A thin, dark girl. She comes in quite a bit. I don't know her name, but I often see her in the park. We sometimes walk along together with our dogs – I can tell you, she's got that picture just right."

Lizzie gulped. "Which park?" she asked, trying not to sound too excited.

Westerly Park is a large place. It has a boating pond, a children's playground, and a rough area like a common that stretches for a kilo-metre or so. It was not an easy place to find anyone in. It was also the other side of town from where Lizzie lived.

For the first two afternoons, it was raining hard. Bella and Lizzie hung around miserably under the shelter of the bandstand. Lizzie was in such state of nerves that she began to wheeze, and Bella made her go home.

The third day was different. Bright and dry, a warm sun made people smile and call out to each other as they walked.

"All right? Lovely day, isn't it?"

"Lovely – 'bout time too."

Lizzie kept telling the butterflies in her stomach to keep quiet, but it was no good. Every time she turned a corner they flew up again.

Then it happened.

"Oh! Look, Lizzie." Lizzie followed Bella's finger. "Fug! Is Fug!"

Hannah was sitting on a bench in the sunshine. The paths here weren't tarmacked, just paths in the long grass. Hannah looked down, laughing at Vanilla, who was lying on her back chewing Hannah's foot.

"Go on, kill it!" Hannah said, wriggling her toes so that the puppy got more and more excited.

Suddenly, quite nearby, two people appeared as if from nowhere. Hannah started nervously until she saw it was only a girl her own age and a young woman. Something made her look up again. The girl was staring at Vanilla as if she had never seen a dog in her life before. Staring and staring. Then, with a horrible lurch, Hannah knew.

"Oh!" said the girl. She was fat, with a pale puffy face, and wore clothes in a style rather too young for her. Hannah hated her immediately.

"Vanilla, come on girl, we're going now." But as she bent to put on her lead, Vanilla shot off. Hannah ran after her.

"Vanilla! Vanilla! Come on, you naughty girl."

Vanilla raced up to Lizzie, and threw herself into the girl's open arms. She was bouncing, licking, whining in excitement. She was beside herself with joy. Then she ran back to Hannah: she seemed to be saying, "Look, Hannah, please come, look who I've found! Isn't it wonderful?" Hannah didn't think so. She tried to grab her, but failed, and the puppy wheeled back to Lizzie again.

Tears ran down Lizzie's face. The puppy licked them off, and wriggled into Lizzie's glad arms. Lizzie knelt, holding her. She had imagined this meeting so many times; she had even worried that Fudge would not recognize her. Of course she would! Now all that remained was to tell this girl the truth and take the puppy back to her true home.

"You've got my—" began Lizzie. But Hannah cut her short.

"I'm sorry my puppy has been troubling you," she said coldly. She snapped the lead on to Vanilla's collar and began to walk away as fast as she could. Lizzie followed, frantic. This wasn't supposed to happen!

"She's not your puppy, she's mine! She recognized me. You saw that."

"Is true, is Fug!" Bella confirmed.

Hannah ignored them and walked faster. She kept the puppy right beside her on a short lead.

"Give her back!" Lizzie said, but Hannah looked away. She was almost running now and Lizzie was struggling to keep up.

"She's my puppy. If you don't give her back this minute I'm going to call the police," Lizzie said furiously. She was beginning to wheeze now, Hannah noticed. She was terrified by the word "police" but she wouldn't slow down.

The puppy trotted joyously between them, blissfully unaware of the flaming row going on over her head.

"Where did you get her?" Lizzie demanded.

"I bought her – fair and square. I bought her from some boys," Hannah said.

"They stole her! They stole her from my house," Lizzie answered in triumph.

"You can't prove it."

"I've got her papers at home. I can prove it. And she was mine first, so you've got to give her back." Lizzie knew she was winning now.

They were near home now, and Hannah wondered what she should do. If they went to her flat, Lizzie would know where she lived – but where else could she go? Feeling for the key in her pocket, Hannah sprinted the last bit and she and the puppy were into the flat in seconds.

She was shaking all over, and furious with Vanilla. "How can you be such a creep?" she scolded the puppy. "How can you like someone so – so fat and ugly? Sometimes I hate you!"

Vanilla looked up with her head on one side, liquid brown eyes troubled. Then her head whipped round to face the door, and she ran up to it with her tail wagging. Hannah looked on in horror: Lizzie was shouting through the letterbox.

"I'm going to phone the police!" she yelled, and Hannah quaked. "And," added Lizzie nastily, "I expect they'll arrest you. I expect it was you who stole her. They won't believe some rubbishy story about boys!"

Hannah shut Vanilla in her bedroom, then jumped on the sofa with her hands over her ears. It was too horrible to bear.

Chapter 12

Lizzie knew the telephone number of the local police station by heart now. A feeling of triumph swelled in her; she didn't feel sorry for Hannah one bit. If Hannah wouldn't give up Fudge, then she, Lizzie, was jolly well going to have to *make* her.

But Lizzie got a nasty shock.

"Can't do, I'm afraid."

"What do you mean, you can't do it?"

"If this girl bought the dog from the boys, legally we can't get it back."

"But Fudge was stolen!"

"Sorry. In British law, once stolen property has been sold, the original owner no longer has any claim to it."

Lizzie was babbling now. "Maybe she was lying. I bet she knew. I bet she did steal Fudge – and do the burglary."

The policeman gave a sour laugh. "No, I think she was telling the truth – it all fits in with what we know already. I know it's rough for you," he added more kindly. "But I'm afraid you'd better give up any hope of getting the pup back."

Lizzie put the phone down shakily. She still couldn't believe it. After all that effort trying to find Fudge and then – then this! It seemed so unfair. Lizzie hated Hannah from the depths of her heart.

Yet she couldn't stop seeing Fudge. Though it was torture to her she made Bella take her to where she could see the puppy. Every day she was drawn like a magnet to the area where Hannah lived and the park she walked Fudge in.

"Is not good to see her," Bella said. "Is making it much badder for you."

But Lizzie pleaded with her and Bella gave in.

Hannah, meanwhile, tried to ignore Lizzie. Whenever she saw her she moved away fast. But Fudge wouldn't ignore her: she was so delighted to see Lizzie. Her tail wagged so hard it seemed it might fall off, and when Hannah went too far she whined anxiously. Hannah was forced to move in circles, not too near, not too far from Lizzie.

Then, on the fourth day, something happened. This time Hannah went up to Lizzie as soon as she saw her. Her face was chalk-white, and her voice was stiff.

"Mum says I've got to give Vanilla back to you."

"What?" Lizzie gaped. She saw that Hannah's eyes were red and puffy, and knew it was true.

Lizzie should have felt simple happiness: she was going to have Fudge back after all. It was wonderful! But suddenly something happened to Lizzie. Suddenly she realized what Hannah must be feeling. She remembered what she had gone through herself and guessed Hannah must be feeling much the same... And that beautiful drawing in the library: it could only have been done by someone who loved Fudge – perhaps as well as she did.

Hannah was talking. All the way here she had been working on an idea – a last, desperate chance to keep the puppy. She must make Lizzie agree! After all, if Lizzie really loved Vanilla, she would want what the puppy wanted.

"I think we should let Vanilla – or Fudge, if you like – decide for herself. I own her now in law, only my mum says I've got to give her back to you. But doesn't Vanilla have rights too?"

Vanilla was chewing Lizzie's hand, while with the other, Lizzie fondled her ears.

"How do you mean?" Lizzie asked.

"I think we should have a – a sort of duel. Let Vanilla choose which one of us she wants."

"That sounds fair," said Lizzie with some reluctance. Hannah pressed her point.

"It *is* fair – nothing could be fairer. If we really, truly want what Vanilla wants then we should do it."

"OK," said Lizzie.

"Tomorrow then?"

"Tomorrow."

Chapter 13

The following day was clear and bright. They should have met at dawn, because Hannah said that was the correct time for duels, but Bella refused to get up so early. The duel was set for nine o'clock.

Neither Hannah nor Lizzie slept that night, but each was quietly sure she would win.

Hannah had been practising calling Vanilla to her for weeks and Vanilla was pretty good at it now. She knew that when Lizzie had had the puppy it was too young to train – Vanilla couldn't possibly go to Lizzie. But Vanilla could sometimes be naughty. Could she be sure? At the corner shop, Hannah bought fifty grammes of aniseed balls and put them in her pocket where the smell would surely be carried on to her hands: dogs were supposed to find aniseed irresistible. "I did want some anyway," Hannah told herself. But it wasn't true – she would never have bought aniseed balls for herself. Hannah was really cheating.

Lizzie wished she hadn't agreed to a duel, but she couldn't get out of it now. She let Hannah take Fudge home that night because she reckoned that Fudge would rush to greet her, and not go to Hannah. But she had no qualms about putting a piece of raw steak in her pocket. It felt horrid, and she knew she would get into trouble with Bella over it – for giving her extra washing and, worse, taking what was supposed to be their supper that night. Well, too bad: this was an emergency.

As Lizzie was getting ready, the phone rang. It was Mr Aubrey. He or Mrs Aubrey often rang, just to see how she was, or to have a chat.

"I'm coming back tomorrow, just for the day."

"What, all that way, just for one day? Is Mum coming?"

"No, just me, I'm afraid. She'll be coming back soon anyway. I'm going to have to stay on. There are complications... I've got – there's something I have to speak to you about."

Lizzie had her mind on other things. "Oh, good," she said, without thinking too much about it. She looked at her watch: it was half-past eight. "I have to go, Dad," she said. "I'll see you tomorrow."

She and Bella raced to the park and arrived at two minutes to nine. Hannah was already there, frowning at her watch.

Hannah had written out the rules carefully on a bit of paper. She read them out in her thin, clear voice. One or two people stopped to watch but when some children ran into the duelling area, Bella shooed them away.

The two girls would stand forty paces apart, with Bella in the middle holding the puppy. Then, when they were ready, Bella would give the signal and let go.

Neither Lizzie nor Hannah was allowed to move, but they would each call the puppy's name. Whichever of them she ran to would be the winner, and the puppy's owner. Bella was the judge, and the judge's decision was final.

"Are you ready?" Hannah asked, and Bella nodded. The puppy wriggled, but Bella held her firm.

"Twenty paces then," said Hannah. They counted out the twenty paces and turned to face each other. They were both pale, and Lizzie was wheezing slightly. She prayed she didn't have an attack of asthma – not now, not here.

Bella looked at both the girls to check they were ready. First one and then the other nodded.

"Now!" Bella said, and let go.

"Vanilla!" Hannah called. Just then, a high-speed plane flew overhead. The puppy cowered and looked up. Lizzie seized her advantage.

"Here, Fudge, come on girl."

Now Hannah called, now Lizzie. The puppy took a few steps towards Hannah and stood with her head on one side. Two people calling her at once; she knew something was expected of her, but what?

Lizzie wanted to scream "Don't, don't!" but she knew it was no good: she had to remain calm.

"Please, Fudge, please," she called. The steak didn't seem to be working; perhaps she was just too far away.

Hannah had sneakily managed things so

that she was upwind of the puppy. She popped an aniseed ball in her mouth and breathed out hopefully. But the wind had dropped. Perhaps she shouldn't have fed Vanilla? Maybe she wasn't hungry?

The puppy moved another step towards Hannah.

"Here, Vanilla, good girl!" Hannah tried to sound encouraging: she was winning! Vanilla was coming towards her and not to Lizzie.

The puppy stopped. For a moment she

turned to Lizzie. Lizzie put out her hand, willing Fudge to her.

But Fudge came to neither. Instead, she squatted down, strained … and then ran off after a small boy.

The two girls were left staring at a fresh, steaming dog dropping. Fudge had made her opinion very clear.

Hannah said sadly, "I suppose you'd better have her."

She's nice, Lizzie thought suddenly. What a shame they had to be enemies. She said awkwardly, "Keep her till the weekend. To get used to the idea."

"Oh!" Hannah saw how much it cost Lizzie to give her this time. She guessed how anxiously the other girl had been waiting for this moment. She wanted to put her arm round Lizzie and thank her like a friend, but it didn't seem the right thing to do. Instead she blushed. "Thank you. Really," she said.

For the first time, she let Lizzie cuddle the puppy without jealousy.

"Till the weekend, then."

"Till the weekend," said Lizzie. "And – sorry."

Chapter 14

Three days. Two days. One day.

On Friday Hannah took Vanilla for a last walk in the park. The puppy seemed to know something was going to happen, for she was particularly affectionate towards Hannah. She didn't run off as usual but stuck to Hannah's side like a young foal. Several times she jumped up with her front paws on Hannah's stomach and looked into Hannah's eyes as if trying to comfort her.

"Don't, Vanilla, please," Hannah said. "You're going to a good home." But she felt terrible. She thought of the lonely summer holidays ahead, her mother busy. She had

planned so many things she and Vanilla would do together. Now she wondered what she would do with herself all that time.

She took Vanilla's head in her hands and fondled the silky brown ears.

Suddenly she could bear it no longer. Maybe she had taken leave of her senses, maybe it was because she was desperate.

"Vanilla," she said. "I've decided I can't let you go. We're going to have to run away." Vanilla licked her hand. Wrongly, Hannah took this to be agreement. She had no clear idea of where she would go, or what she would do when she got there. She would go tonight – Lizzie would just have to lump it.

But at that moment Hannah looked up and saw Lizzie coming towards her. Lizzie was the last person she wanted to see just then. Worse still, Lizzie looked angry.

Hannah was alarmed. Could Lizzie have guessed and come to take Vanilla early? She tried to hide, but it was too late. Lizzie had seen her.

"Tomorrow," Hannah said. "It's supposed to be tomorrow – at my house." But Lizzie didn't even hear her.

"I hate you!" she cried, and Hannah shrank back. Lizzie's face was curled in anger but suddenly it collapsed like a puppet with cut strings.

"It's happened again," she sobbed. "Every time I think I'm going to get Fudge back, something happens. It's – just so unfair! And this is it. This is the end."

"What's happened? What's the end?"

"Dad came back today. He's been out in

Germany – he came back specially to tell me something. Mum wanted to come but he said I'd be too cross with her. And I am," Lizzie added fiercely. "You know I get asthma?"

Hannah nodded.

"It's in the family – allergies, I mean. Mum and I are both allergic to cats. Since Fudge came, Mum had been having these awful headaches. We thought nothing of it – usually she just gets hayfever. Only she went and had these special tests and it turns out she's badly allergic to dogs."

"So they said you couldn't keep Vanilla – Fudge – after all?"

Lizzie wiped her nose on her sleeve and sniffed. "Yes."

Hannah was stricken with guilt. Almost under her breath, she said, "I was going to run away."

"Run away?" said Lizzie. "Where to?"

"I – didn't really know," Hannah admitted. "London probably."

Lizzie looked shocked at first. Then she said cautiously, "Do you think we could run away together? Would you mind having me along?"

Hannah was uncertain. She didn't need to run away at all now. Only Lizzie was looking at her so earnestly. Guilt won.

"All right," she said weakly.

When Lizzie decided to do something she did it. Her mind was rolling furiously. "I don't think London would be good – they're bound to look for us there. Anyway, it's no good for dogs."

"I hadn't thought of that," Hannah said, ashamed.

For a while neither of them spoke. They sat and watched the puppy, who was running round in circles with her nose to the ground. Lizzie couldn't stop going over and over the conversation she'd just had with her father. The first thing she'd said, before he told her about Fudge, was, "How is Mr Barbed Wire? What's he like?" And Mr Aubrey had groaned, and said, "Not an easy man to get along with."

But thinking about Mr Barbed Wire made Lizzie remember Uncle Ralph. "Got it!" she said. "Uncle Ralph's cottage! He doesn't go there that often, 'cause it's so far from London. He always says he likes it being used. It's perfect!"

Hannah began to be more enthusiastic. "How do we get there?" she asked.

"Oh, that's simple. There's a train most of the way, and then we take a bus. I did it with my last au-pair. And Daddy left loads of money for Bella to take me places. I've some saved too."

They walked together back to Hannah's flat, planning all the way.

"We should swear an oath to secrecy!" Hannah said, and Lizzie agreed. They also decided that from now on the puppy would be called "Vanilla Fudge". As Lizzie pointed out, "It gets in both her colours, so really it's a better name."

Ruth Wilder, when she had recovered from the shock of seeing the girls so friendly together, insisted Lizzie phone Bella.

"Ooops!" Lizzie said. "I forgot to tell her I'd gone out."

Hannah's mother looked at them suspiciously: there was something going on between those two...

Chapter 15

She was still surprised when, the following day, a letter came from Lizzie's mother, asking Hannah to come and stay at their country cottage in Cornwall.

The letter was beautifully typed out on a computer, and went a long way to making her feel more comfortable about her precious daughter going to visit people she hardly knew. Hannah's blushes she put down to pleasure.

"I'll ring and thank her," she said.

But the conversation she had with Bella was rather confused.

"Mrs Aubrey is not here. Has holiday. Thank you for holiday, for Lizzie is loving it."

"I think I should be thanking you," Ruth Wilder said. "So Mrs Aubrey is already there, is she?"

"Yes, Mrs Aubrey haves holiday. Thank you too."

What Hannah's mother didn't know was that Bella had received a similar letter, supposedly from herself. In truth it was also typed out by Lizzie. This one was rather less well written because Lizzie had not been able to use the prepared layout that her father used for his own letters. But Bella didn't notice spelling mistakes in the address or a missing full stop; she was so glad the girls were friends.

It was difficult not to be carried along by Lizzie. Hannah felt terrible at first about tricking her mother, but Lizzie said, "Well, it's sort of true – we are going away together." She brandished a pair of scissors. "I've had another idea. So's they don't find us we'll disguise ourselves as boys."

"Cut our hair, you mean?"

*   *   *

Ssscrick! An electric thrill ran down Hannah's spine as she held all of Lizzie's fair wavy hair and sliced through the lot. Lizzie laughed to see how it stuck out now, much longer on one side than the other. But that was only the start... Hannah chopped at it again – then more, and more.

"It's got to be really short," insisted Lizzie, "or people won't believe us."

Hannah being artistic, it was Lizzie who got the best cut. They admired themselves in front of the mirror. It was astonishing how different they looked – you would never guess they were girls.

Hannah felt rather peculiar. Had Lizzie really needed to give her a crew-cut?

"Look," Lizzie said. She puffed out her chest and stuck out her lower lip, tough-guy style. She looked absolutely terrifying, and they burst into fits of giggles.

Half an hour later, Hannah pulled out the travel bag she had hidden under Lizzie's bed and they crept out of the house.

They were in high spirits. Lizzie played the boy, kicking out at stones and whistling at pictures of women. Vanilla Fudge knew something was happening. She pulled this way and that, letting out little barks of excitement.

At the station, Lizzie decided to buy some sweets. But as they went into the shop, Hannah pulled Lizzie back. "Wait!"

"What's the matter?"

Hannah waited until they were far enough from any prying ears.

"We're boys, remember? We can't call each other by our real names. We'll have to think some up."

"Oh! Thank goodness you thought of it in time."

"What are you going to be?"

Lizzie's mind was a complete blank. She couldn't use her father's name; that would be a giveaway. What about Grandad's? "Er ... Francis!"

Hannah giggled. "That's hopeless: it's a

girl's name too. Think of some of the boys in your class."

"William. James – eugh! Not him. Abdul … Dylan! I'll be Dylan," she decided.

"And I'll be – if I was a boy, Mum was going to call me Michael, so I'll be that – Mike for short." Freshly decorated with boy's names, the two girls entered the shop. Hannah shrank from calling out "Dylan" every time she spoke to Lizzie; she was sure the woman in the shop would guess. Lizzie, however, enjoyed herself.

"Hey, cool, look at these football cards, Mike!" And: "Oh, Mike, do you like salt 'n' vinegar crisps?"

"Yes!" squeaked Hannah, and blushed purple.

Fortunately the woman noticed nothing.

On the train they didn't talk much in case anyone was listening. Hannah read, though she was too excited to take in much. Lizzie walked Vanilla Fudge up and down to calm her. After a bit they all fell asleep.

They woke with a jolt when the train stopped, and managed to get their things together just in time.

Hannah looked about her. They were in a small station in a grey, ugly town. But the air smelt sweet, and in the distance she could see the huge grey shapes of mountains. It was a holiday area, and the platform was filled with tired parents trying to carry impossibly large suitcases and wildly excited children. No one took any notice of them.

Lizzie led them over a footbridge to the bus station. Everything so far had gone right, and they felt both happy and proud: they were having a real adventure.

Hannah decoded the bus timetable. "I'm afraid there isn't a bus for three hours," she said.

Lizzie looked worried. "It'll be dark when we get there," she said.

By this time, only Hannah had a sandwich left. She broke it in two and shared it: it wasn't much. Lizzie wanted to buy some milk for Vanilla Fudge but the station café was closed and she had to eat dry food. They did get water for her by bringing it from the Ladies' Cloakroom in cupped hands.

Three hours is a long time when you are tired. Vanilla Fudge hated being on a lead all that time, and kept trying to pull it out of their hands.

"It's only because we don't want you to get run over," Lizzie told her. Vanilla Fudge lay with her nose between her paws and sulked.

At last the bus arrived. It must have been market day, for suddenly people carrying bags of shopping appeared from nowhere and began to fill it with alarming speed. They had to push to get on at all.

Chapter 16

Safe beneath the roar of the engine, Lizzie told Hannah all about the cottage. Hannah was struck by her account of the mysterious Mr Barbed Wire.

"At the village shop they say he's in antiques – but then what does he want with my father?" Lizzie said.

"I bet he's not really called 'Smith' either," Hannah said. "They always say they're called Smith."

"Who's 'they'?"

"Criminals, of course. Promise we go and look at his place tomorrow?" Hannah said. Lizzie was feeling decidedly uncomfortable.

"My dad isn't a criminal," she said hotly.

"Oh…" Hannah saw she had been tactless. "Sorry, I didn't mean … only…" Lizzie cut her short.

"It's our stop."

"It's pitch black," Hannah said. "I hope you know the way," she added with a wobble in her voice.

Lizzie tried to make sense of the shapes that loomed up round them. She waited until their eyes were used to the dark. They were in a narrow lane that sloped upward to a wood. At some distance you could just make out a sprinkling of lights.

"That's the village," she said with some relief. "I think this is the right way." She led Hannah back along the road a little, over a stone stile and down a steep, muddy track. Although it wasn't actually raining all the plants seemed to be reaching out wet hands towards them. It felt rather creepy. They went down and down. Every time they came to a stile, Vanilla Fudge had to be lifted over, and each time she was muddier.

"We're going past Mr Barbed Wire's place now. That's the gate in – and that track goes up to the road we came on," Lizzie said. Hannah peered in the direction Lizzie pointed but she could see nothing.

At last Lizzie said: "We're here!" Hannah almost burst with relief.

Lizzie felt for the key in a pot and opened the cottage door. A smell of damp billowed out. She turned on a light, and they looked at one another in triumph. They had really arrived.

But the long day was not over yet. Suddenly they were both aware of how cold they were – and wet. When Lizzie had arrived here before, it had been lovely and warm – probably someone from the village had come in and built a fire. Now the cottage was almost as cold inside as out.

"Shall we just go to bed?" Hannah said. She was too tired to be hungry.

But when they got upstairs, the two beds were bare. Lizzie and Hannah stared at them

in dismay. Was this expedition such a good idea after all?

"Where are the sheets kept?" Hannah said in a stiff voice.

"I don't know," Lizzie said miserably. The duvets were folded on the ends of the beds. "Shall we just go to bed as we are?"

"We'll make the duvets muddy," Hannah said.

Lizzie was too tired to care. "So what?" she said savagely.

There was only one good thing about that night. Halfway through it, Lizzie woke with a squeal; something cold was poking her. It was Vanilla Fudge. Lizzie reached down and pulled her on to the bed, where she snuggled up to Lizzie with squeaks of pleasure. It was worth everything, just for this, Lizzie thought – having Fudge on her bed had never been allowed at home.

Chapter 17

Hannah sat up in bed and winced: a shaft of sunlight had danced across her eyes and woken her up. Remembering where she was she leaped up and ran over bare boards to the window.

It was wonderful! They were in a narrow valley on the slopes of a large mountain. On one side a scattering of trees followed a stream down in a wiggly line.

Behind her, Vanilla Fudge yawned and stretched, and burrowed under the bed-clothes to wake Lizzie.

"What can we do about food?" Hannah wondered. She was suddenly ravenous.

"Oh, there's stacks in the larder," Lizzie said. "We'll go to the shop later for fresh stuff."

"Isn't it stealing?" Hannah worried.

Lizzie opened the freezer and pulled out a loaf of bread, knocking it expertly on the stone floor to free the slices. "They wouldn't want us to starve, would they?" In a cupboard she found long-life milk and cereal.

Hannah was not completely satisfied by Lizzie's explanation. "Well, we must at least buy some dog food," she said, watching Lizzie open a tin of steak and kidney for Vanilla Fudge. Vanilla Fudge looked as if she might disagree.

They ate their breakfast at a wooden table, just outside the back door, and breathed in the sour-sweet smells of bracken and wild thyme steaming off the mountain. Vanilla Fudge trotted round the garden until she fell asleep in Hannah's lap. Everything seemed perfect. Neither of the girls thought for a moment about home or parents.

"Shall we have a fire this evening?" Lizzie pointed her piece of toast in the direction of a pile of wood under a lean-to shelter.

"Ooh, yes," said Hannah. "It was so cold last night."

Lizzie stuffed the last piece of toast in her mouth and jumped up. "We'll have to chop it smaller or it won't go in the fireplace – and we'll need some kindling." She took an axe from where it hung on the wall and handled it doubtfully.

"I haven't chopped wood before but I remember how Dad did it. You've got to be careful you don't chop your own legs."

"You go first," Hannah said nervously. She backed away as Lizzie swung the axe. She was wobbly at first, and kept missing the log. After some effort they both managed the axe quite well. They were very proud when they at last had wood enough to fill two baskets.

That day they didn't go far – there was too much to do around the cottage. They found some sheets and Lizzie made her own bed for the first time in her life.

"Huh!" scoffed Hannah at Lizzie's lop-sided effort. "It'll all get screwed up and keep you awake if you leave it like that. Come on, I'll help you get it better."

"What can we eat for supper?" Lizzie wondered.

Hannah inspected larder and freezer. Meat in freezer … onions, garlic hanging up. Most of the onions were soft, but two were all right. The garlic was fine.

"What about spaghetti bolognese?"

"Make it ourselves, do you mean? Do you know how?"

"It's easy," Hannah said.

"Really?" Lizzie was terribly impressed. Under Hannah's guidance she wept over onions, peeled garlic and stirred the savoury mess until it appeared on their plates in a swirl of mouthwatering steam.

Lizzie was full to bursting, and bursting with pride. "What else can we cook?"

"I don't know much else, but I saw some cookery books on the kitchen shelf – I'm sure we could find things that wouldn't be too hard."

They sat in front of the fire (which took seven firelighters and most of the kindling to light) and pored over the books until they were too sleepy to stay awake any longer.

Chapter 18

In the village shop next morning, Hannah wasn't nearly as scared at being found out. In fact she rather enjoyed arguing with her mate "Dylan" over a box of firelighters.

After that they went out to explore, taking a picnic lunch. Vanilla Fudge couldn't believe her luck. She raced round in circles, every now and then letting out a little bark of joy. Sometimes she went so fast she couldn't stop, rolling over and over until she jumped up and shook herself in surprise.

Up and up they climbed until they left the fields behind them and were out on open moorland.

Hannah had never been to Wales: she noticed all sorts of flowers and birds she hadn't seen before. A huge hawk eyed them from high in the air and Hannah watched it back with equal interest. "I must bring my sketch book next time," she said.

Lizzie knew where she was going. As they passed a fallen tree she turned aside and headed for a funny-shaped rock sticking out of the bracken. She pointed down.

"Look, Mr Barbed Wire's place," she said. Hannah scrambled up beside her. "It's the only place you can see the house," Lizzie explained. "Lower down there are trees in the way – you can't even see the fence from here."

Hannah saw a grey house with high windows, and a tall bit one end, making it look like a very small church.

"That's what it used to be – a chapel. It was all falling down when Mr Barbed Wire bought it. They think he must be mad in the village – buying something like that when there were plenty of perfectly good places much easier to get to." Behind the house were

some concrete outbuildings. There were no
people in view and it all looked very dead and
dull.

"Isn't that our cottage – I mean your
uncle's – behind it?" She was surprised at
how near it was. Mr Barbed Wire didn't have
such a big place then – just a few hectares.
Millions of years ago there had been a lake:
now it was just a small woody area tucked into
the mountainside.

"Yes," Lizzie said. "We'll have to go back
that way."

"Oh good." Hannah was pleased – she wanted to have a closer look. Going down it was so steep they had to sit on their bottoms most of the way. Vanilla Fudge was careful too; she'd had enough somersaults for one day.

"If she tripped here she'd roll all the way to Mr Barbed Wire's," Hannah said, watching her zig-zag back and forth.

They reached the bottom and joined the footpath running through a little wood and along the edge of Mr Barbed Wire's land. By daylight Hannah was even more puzzled by the high fence of metal and barbed wire: so odd right in the middle of the country. Next to the fence, all the way round, a narrow belt of grass was kept short by sheep, who looked up at them curiously. Just then, Vanilla Fudge sprang to attention and trotted up to the fence. They followed the direction of her nose. About fifty metres away, in the shrubbery, a man had appeared. He was staring at them. Dressed in army-type greens, he almost disappeared in the shadows. His legs were apart and his elbows raised to shoulder height: a gun! thought Hannah with a lurch of fear. The man shifted slightly and sunlight caught twin globes of light: not a gun then, but binoculars.

Beside her, Lizzie tugged at her sleeve. "I don't like it. Let's go home." Hannah shivered and nodded.

Lizzie kept thinking back to what Hannah had said on the bus. Why would an ordinary antique dealer need barbed wire fencing and a guard with binoculars? Perhaps Mr Smith really was a criminal. Of course her dad wasn't one – but what did Mr "Smith" Barbed Wire really do? And what was Mr Aubrey doing for Mr Barbed Wire?

Hannah said: "I'm sorry – about what I said on the bus. Are you worried about your dad?"

Lizzie nodded.

"I'm sure there's an explanation. You know all about computers. Aren't computers used when they X-ray old paintings to see if there's another picture underneath? Computers make the fuzzy X-ray picture better –

'computer enhanced'. Maybe that's it? P'raps we've just been watching too much telly."

"Yes. Maybe," said Lizzie. She smiled at Hannah awkwardly. "Thanks."

Chapter 19

The days passed and each one was better than the last. They went for long walks on the mountain, eating when they felt like it, and coming back when they felt like it. It was wonderful not to have grown-ups always telling you to stop because it is time for this or that. Sometimes they played in the stream, jumping from rock to rock, or making little dams or waterfalls. In the evenings they always ate supper in front of the fire. Sometimes they talked long into the night.

"Tell me again about when you went to buy Vanilla Fudge." Or: "What did you really feel when you saw those boys pulling her along?"

They had become expert by now at chopping wood – though Lizzie was the best.

On some parts of the mountain there were sheep grazing. At first, Vanilla Fudge was terrified – she leapt into the air and hid behind Hannah. The girls laughed. But one day she began to bark at one: the sheep raced off, and Vanilla Fudge shot after it with a look of surprised joy.

"Quick!" Lizzie shouted. "We've got to stop her!"

"She won't do it any harm." Hannah was enjoying it almost as much as the puppy – the sheep was so much larger and it looked so funny with its great woolly body and stick legs.

The sheep had joined up with a lot of others and they bobbed about on the hillside like balls of crazy candyfloss. Vanilla Fudge didn't know which one to chase, dashing after first one, then another.

"Come on!" Lizzie said urgently and Hannah caught the sound of fear in her voice.

Lizzie couldn't run as fast as Hannah and she was beginning to wheeze. The sheep were calling to one another in high, frightened tones. Suddenly one raced towards Lizzie, Vanilla Fudge hot on its heels, head and tail held high. With an enormous effort Lizzie flung her down in a rugby tackle. The puppy squealed in shock – but Lizzie had her firmly round the collar. She was dizzy with relief and panting hard when Hannah trotted up, a little puzzled at all the fuss.

"She's only little – she wouldn't hurt them," Hannah said.

"Uncle Ralph told me that farmers are allowed to shoot dogs that chase sheep."

"Shoot them!" Hannah was horrified. "How horrible of them."

"No, no," Lizzie said. "All dogs have a bit of the wild animal in them; they can't help it. They just get excited. Even if they don't bite, just chasing sheep can kill them sometimes. If they are pregnant it can kill their lambs too."

"Oh!" Hannah wished she had moved faster now. She imagined Vanilla Fudge all

limp and covered in blood. She shuddered. "What should we do?"

"We'll have to train her. It won't be easy now she's seen how much fun it is to chase things."

So several times a day they spent a few minutes giving Vanilla Fudge obedience lessons. They taught her to sit, to stay and always to come when she was called. "Not just when she feels like it," as Lizzie said. It was much easier to train her when there were two of them – there was always one to give the command and the other to make sure she did it. And (with the help of Happi-Chum chocolate drops) Vanilla Fudge proved a good pupil.

Lizzie was getting stronger; there was no doubt about it. On the first day she was wheezing after only a few minutes' climbing. Hannah had had to keep stopping to let her catch her breath. Now she could walk miles without even thinking.

One day the two girls had been out all day, swimming in a pool they had found. They were nearly home, passing Mr Barbed Wire's land. They were just picking their way through a boggy stream when Hannah noticed the puppy wasn't with them.

"Where's Vanilla Fudge?"

They went back the way they had come, listening, calling her name. But no puppy came.

"Maybe she went after a rabbit." Lizzie tried not to sound worried.

Suddenly Hannah cried. "There she is!" But their relief was short-lived. Vanilla Fudge was on the wrong side of the fence. She was in Mr Barbed Wire's land.

"How on earth did she get there?" Hannah gasped. Suddenly she realized why Mr Barbed Wire kept sheep on that narrow belt of land – anyone who did get past the fence would be easily seen by the man with binoculars: Vanilla Fudge stuck out like a traffic light. And what would the man do if he did find her?

Lizzie was more worried about something else.

"The sheep. We've got to get her out before she sees them."

She was right; no dog is perfectly trained after only a few days. And Vanilla Fudge was very young. They looked at one another in horror. The fence was impossibly high, the wire barbs sharp and cruel.

"Could we climb it if we drape our clothes over so's we don't get hurt?" Lizzie suggested.

Hannah frowned. "I still don't think we could manage the top bit – not if we were carrying Vanilla Fudge."

At the moment the sheep were some way off. But already one or two had lifted their heads from the grass and were watching the dog suspiciously.

"At least we know the man isn't around yet – the sheep would have noticed him too," Lizzie said. They peered anxiously into the wood.

"How did you get in?" she asked the puppy. Vanilla Fudge whined, and wagged her tail; she had clearly forgotten. Lizzie prayed the sheep would stay quiet – but sheep never stay quiet for long.

What should they do? They walked along the fence a bit, hoping to find the gap she had come in by. But they found nothing. Vanilla Fudge trotted alongside, on the other side of the fence. She was beginning to get bored – it was only a matter of seconds before she ran off. Then she would surely see the sheep.

As they came to a place where the trees were larger, Hannah said, "Look!"

About six feet outside the fence grew an old oak tree. Its trunk was mossy and knotted –

easy to climb. But what Hannah had noticed
was the thick branch that reached out on to
Mr Barbed Wire's land…

Hannah was half-way up the trunk when
Lizzie called out excitedly.

"Hannah!" Hannah looked down, to see a
rather shamefaced Vanilla Fudge sitting
politely at Lizzie's feet.

"She popped out just by my feet," Lizzie
said when Hannah had climbed down. She
showed Hannah the large hole, almost
completely hidden by long grass. "It wasn't a

gap in the fence at all, but an animal hole – a fox or badger sett. It must go right under the fence."

They almost ran home, looking behind them in case anyone was following. Nobody did but they had been badly scared.

That evening neither felt like cooking supper, and they quarrelled.

For the first time, Lizzie began to miss her parents. Every time they passed Mr Barbed Wire's place she was reminded of her father, and the more she thought about it the more uneasy she felt.

Chapter 20

"That was Jack. It wasn't them." Mrs Aubrey sank into a chair. Bella looked on with troubled eyes.

Since the dreadful day she discovered Lizzie was not on holiday with the Wilders, Bella had not slept. None of them had. Mrs Aubrey put the phone down and sat with her head in her hands.

"Another false alarm. Two girls, but not ours... Oh, Bella. What am I going to do?"

Bella put her arms round Mrs Aubrey. "Is my fault, is stupid me," she cried.

If there had been a television in the cottage,

Lizzie and Hannah would have known their trick had been discovered, and at that very moment a nationwide search was out for them. Police in every county were on the alert, and blurred photographs of them had appeared in all the papers – Lizzie on the library steps (looking fatter and very sulky), Hannah cut from a class photograph. But everyone was looking for two girls – not two scruffy, shock-headed boys.

Unaware of all the excitement, Hannah and Lizzie were having their own problems.

"This porridge won't cook," Hannah said crossly.

"I'll take over," Lizzie said. Lizzie who, only a few short months ago, had not known how to boil a kettle. This same Lizzie could now chop wood and light fires with enviable skill. She made a mean spaghetti bolognese, and quite a good chicken and mushroom pie. But not today.

"I can't think what's wrong," she said.

"I know," Hannah said gloomily. "The gas canister's running out." She was right. Within a few minutes, the flame grew more and more feeble. Finally it ran out altogether.

"What do we do now?" They looked at the greyish blobbly mass of half-cooked oats.

"I suppose it's sort of like muesli. Without the nuts and things," Hannah said doubtfully.

Lizzie just screwed up her face. "I'm not eating that."

"How do we get another gas thing?"

But Lizzie didn't know. "They don't sell them in the village shop."

After that things were different. It wasn't nearly so nice now they couldn't cook supper every night. Also, their clothes were beginning to feel very grubby. Up till now they had just dried things over the fire whenever they got wet. Neither troubled to keep anything clean.

There was only a shower in the cottage. Lizzie, who had a bath every night at home, began to think how nice it would be to have one. "A nice hot one, with something smelly in it, and Mum bringing me a huge fluffy towel … and then to Dad's study in my

pyjamas and fiddling about on a computer
with him."

Hannah thought of the sound of her
mother's key turning in the lock, of racing
with the puppy to be the first to greet her.

They began to bicker.

"I washed up last night and the night before
– it's your turn."

"Yes, but I spent ages chopping wood and
lighting the fire."

"Lighting a fire's more fun – try doing
something you don't like for a change."

And then there was money. Lizzie had
brought what seemed like masses… Where
had it gone? There wasn't much left at all.

Then one day Hannah raced into the cottage.
"Quick! We've got to get out!"

Lizzie stared at the frightened face. "What's
happened?" she asked in alarm.

"It's your uncle – I heard in the shop – he's
coming back – this evening!"

For a moment the two looked at each other.

Both longed to see their parents. No more washing up … nice hot meals. Most of all, a good long hug.

"Shall we just…?" Hannah began. Then she stopped. Her eyes moved round the room.

Suddenly Lizzie realized. "Oh, dear." The cottage was a mess. Not just untidy, but awful, dirty.

They cleaned up as best they could, but the effect of two muddy girls and a puppy that chews everything was only too clear.

"We can't let him know it was us," Lizzie said.

"And all that food. It's nearly all gone. What shall we do?"

"We'll have to go … somewhere," Lizzie said. They took the last of the food, leaving what was left of Lizzie's money on the kitchen table, and a note that just said "sorry". Lizzie counted the money out; it wasn't nearly enough.

Outside it was a warm, still afternoon, but to the girls, even the soft hum of insects sounded frightening; they had no idea where they would spend the night.

Chapter 21

"We can't stay out on the mountain," Hannah said with fear. "We'll get exposure."

"What's that?" It sounded awful.

"I don't know really," Hannah said. "It's something you get on mountains. You mustn't go to sleep but you keep wanting to and you get colder and colder. They find you in the morning cold and stiff."

"Dead?"

Hannah nodded. In the distance a diesel engine started up. As it became louder they looked up. Hannah shielded her eyes from the sun as a black four-wheel drive came out of the trees on the other side of the valley.

"Coming from Mr Barbed Wire's place."

Lizzie grabbed her arm. They watched the car slowly ride the bumpy track and move off into the distance.

"Do you think the place is empty now?" Lizzie said. "We could shelter in one of the buildings."

Hannah stared at her. "Inside Mr Barbed Wire's place?"

"We know how to get in now – up that tree."

Suddenly the idea seemed a good one. No one would possibly think of looking for them there – and the thought of being safely inside all that barbed wire was much better than spending a night out on the open mountain.

They hid in the shrubbery until they were quite sure the man with the binoculars was not about. Everything was quiet. Then – Lizzie first while Hannah held Vanilla Fudge, and then Hannah – they climbed inside the fence. Vanilla Fudge slipped in through the badger hole. Hearts in mouths and checking all round they ran towards the buildings.

* * *

But first one door, then another was locked. By the time they got to the fourth they both knew it would be locked: it was a bitter blow.

"What shall we do now?" Lizzie was almost crying with frustration. Hannah shook her head; she couldn't bear to think of climbing out again. They knew there wasn't anywhere sheltered for miles. How about getting in through a window? Hannah crept to one and peered in. It was very dusty; she rubbed at it with a sleeve. "Just a store room," she said. Lizzie looked too: a few garden tools, oil and a rag on a table. She rubbed some more dust away. On the windowsill just in front of her nose was a coffee mug. As she watched, a curl of steam rose into the air and blurred the pane again.

Lizzie stopped what she was doing. If the coffee was hot, someone might still be drinking it! She sank away from the window, pulling Hannah down beside her. Putting a finger in front of her lips, and hauling the puppy along by her collar she didn't explain till they were well away.

"I think someone's in there!"

"Did you see who?"

But Lizzie shook her head.

"Do you think whoever it is saw us?" Hannah spoke fearfully. "I mean we've broken in. We shouldn't be here at all. I wonder what they'd do to us?"

Lizzie tried to be sensible. "It can't be that bad. If Dad's working for Smith he must be all right. Maybe we should just—" She was about to say, "give ourselves up," when Vanilla Fudge stiffened and pricked her ears.

Coming round the end of the building was the binoculars man. He was striding along, the binoculars swinging from his shoulder. He was talking on a mobile phone to someone who seemed very cross. "Yes, sir, I'm sorry. Right away, sir."

It didn't seem a good moment to introduce themselves. Without stopping to think, Hannah picked up Vanilla Fudge and raced round a corner. Lizzie followed. Here the

shrubbery stopped. Where could they hide?

They had arrived at the back of Mr Barbed Wire's house. Lizzie shuddered at the thought of Mr Barbed Wire coming out and finding them – only that was silly. He was hundreds of miles away ... wasn't he?

Behind them, they heard the sound of Binoculars Man. Had he seen them? He was still rather busy with the phone.

"The back door," Hannah whispered. "Quick!"

Lizzie saw where she meant. On the side of

the house, a door was swinging open. Right inside the house? It seemed a bit daring. With Vanilla bouncing up and down in Hannah's arms they ran for it and slipped inside.

They were at the foot of a winding stone staircase. There was nowhere else to go. Round and round, up and up they ran. At the top was a stout wooden door. Hannah hesitated, but Lizzie pushed ahead and opened it. "It's the bell-tower," she said.

Hannah followed her in and closed the door behind them. With beating hearts they listened. Would he come up? Silence. The girls waited. The only noise was their breathing. After a bit Vanilla Fudge wriggled out of Hannah's arms, and Hannah did not try to stop her.

The bell-room was small and square, with a huge wooden beam across where the bell used to hang. Four slit windows each looked out in a different direction across the valley. A large desk stood in one corner, and a hard chair, but nothing else. The room was not comfortable in any way, but it would certainly shelter them from the weather.

"I like his pictures," Hannah said, looking round the walls. "Tunnicliffe is famous for drawing birds."

"Buzzards. There's lots round here," said Lizzie.

"It says 'Kites'." said Hannah.

An hour passed, then another. Vanilla Fudge explored the waste paper basket and chewed (unsuccessfully) a metal chair leg. Then she went to sleep on Hannah's lap.

"I'm bored," Lizzie said.

"Shall we play... My Grandmother's Cat ... or...?"

"No!" said Lizzie grumpily. She was watching Vanilla Fudge, snuffling happily in her sleep.

"Hannah," she said suddenly. "Do you think they'd be very cross if we went back home?"

A great wave of relief washed over Hannah. "But – what about Vanilla Fudge?"

"I – I don't want to think about that," Lizzie said. "But I think perhaps we should. Tomorrow. We could sneak out first thing."

From then on, every moment was special. They saved the food they had brought until it was dark, and ate by moonlight. Later they bedded down on the floor. Although they huddled together with their coats on top, it was rather cold. Vanilla Fudge nudged between them. They were very glad of her company.

Lizzie slept badly. It was uncomfortable on the floor, and rather dusty. Dawn came. It was too early to wake Hannah. She lay half awake,

half asleep and listened to the sounds of birds calling to one another across the valley.

Quite suddenly, she was aware of another noise. Vanilla Fudge jumped up and ran to the door, ears pricked. With a horrid jolt, Lizzie realized what it was. Footsteps! Someone was coming up the stairs. Any moment they would be right inside the room. She shook the bewildered Hannah awake, leapt up, snatched up the puppy and streaked under the desk. She was only just in time.

Two sturdy legs in army greens came into the room. Something clattered on to the table just above their heads. The legs walked over to a window and stood there a moment. The girls froze. Binoculars Man picked whatever it was off the table and walked slowly to the door, holding something low in his hands. At that moment, they saw what it was. Hannah stuffed a hand into her mouth to stop the cry that rose in her throat.

Lizzie's heart was beating so fast it seemed to shake her whole body. A gun! If Mr Smith used guns then they were in real danger. All her fears about Barbed Wire being a criminal came back to her. All that talk about antiques – why, they had seen no sign of that at all. All this secrecy must mean something nasty after all. And Dad! she thought. If they were in danger, what about him? All this time she and Hannah had been enjoying themselves – but how was he? Why was he involved with a man like this? And Mum? Anything could have happened.

"We must get out! We must warn the police." Lizzie's breath came in a wheeze: she hadn't been wheezy for weeks but it always got worse when she was tired or upset. Beside her, Hannah wished she would shut up. Suppose the man heard?

But they had reckoned without Vanilla Fudge…

Chapter 22

Well house-trained by now, the second she saw the door being opened again Vanilla Fudge struggled away and raced to it, anxious not to make a mess.

"What the—?" Binoculars Man almost fell over her.

They heard a yell of surprise as the frightened puppy dodged past him and streaked down the stairs. But they saw nothing of what happened next.

Another man appeared. "What's going on? I saw a dog." It was Mr Smith. He and Binoculars Man tried their best, but five minutes later, Vanilla Fudge had still not been caught.

"Where could it have gone? It can't be far."

Just then Mr Smith gave a shout. "Look!"

The other man stared.

They had found the puppy all right. But she was on the other side of the fence. They walked up and peered through. Vanilla Fudge wagged at them hopefully. But the men were not the slightest bit friendly.

"Must be a gap somewhere." They walked up and down, snarling at the puppy, and very cross indeed. But however hard they looked, they could not find it.

Feeling sadly deserted, Vanilla Fudge sat down and howled plaintively. She waited to see if Lizzie or Hannah might come, then, the picture of misery, she trotted away.

Binoculars Man muttered to himself gloomily: he knew the boss would give him big trouble over a dog getting in.

"I've seen it before," he said. "With a couple of boys."

"Boys? Search the place," Mr Smith ordered. "I don't expect it came alone."

*　　*　　*

It was not long before Hannah and Lizzie were hauled out. Binoculars Man stood in the doorway and called down.

"I've got them, sir. Two boys. They were in the bell-room."

An angry voice yelled. "Lock 'em in. Let them stew a bit. I don't care."

"But sir, they're only kids. Shouldn't we—"

The angry voice got even angrier.

"Yes, sir, of course, sir." Binoculars Man turned to the two girls. "Right. Back in there. Mr Smith will speak to you later."

Shut up in the bell-room, Lizzie and Hannah were very frightened indeed.

Hannah stood by a window and watched three hawks lazily circling high in the air, round and round. They are free, she thought. We are prisoners.

"What do you think Mr Barbed Wire is going to do with us?" she said.

"I don't know," Lizzie said shakily. She couldn't stop thinking about the gun. She wished Vanilla Fudge were still there. Where was Vanilla Fudge?

* * *

The breakfast Binoculars Man brought them was surprisingly good – steaming hot chocolate, bacon, eggs and toast. Lizzie couldn't eat much, but Hannah wolfed it down. Then she had a sudden worry. "I suppose it's not … poisoned," she said.

Just then, Binoculars Man came back. "The boss'll see you now," he said. "And you'll have to watch it: he's not too pleased with you."

Pale and trembling, the two girls were pushed in front of Mr Smith.

Hannah gulped with fear. How were they going to get out of this? Binoculars Man went quietly out, and they were quite alone with Mr Smith.

Mr Smith sat in an armchair and looked the two up and down coldly. He was not large and fearsome as Hannah had expected; quite the opposite in fact. But there was no kindness in his pale eyes.

"What are your names?" he said. "Quickly now."

"Mike," said Hannah bravely.

"Um…" In her panic, Lizzie couldn't think. And she really wasn't feeling well. "Abdul."

"Abdul! A likely story." His eyes stung into her. Lizzie looked down and said nothing.

"And why did you choose the bell-room?"

"We needed shelter, sir," Hannah answered.

"Hah!" Mr Smith tossed his head in disbelief. "Watching. Waiting till we got out of the way – weren't you?" he suddenly snapped at Lizzie. Lizzie didn't know what to do. She just nodded.

Hannah could see how scared she was. "I'm

sorry sir," she said. "We didn't mean any harm."

But Mr Smith ignored her. He kept his gaze firmly on Lizzie. "Thieving. Weren't you?"

"Oh, no," Lizzie said. Her breath came in a rasp.

Hannah suddenly remembered the hawks, and the pictures on the walls. She had a brainwave. "We were birdwatching," she said.

But for some reason this made Mr Barbed Wire absolutely wild. He steamed with rage. "Come on now. I want the truth! You're lying."

Just then, there was a knock at the door, and Binoculars Man put his head nervously round the door.

"Sir... It's the police, sir."

Mr Barbed Wire said crossly, "But I told you not yet."

"No, sir, they just came. They think we might have a couple of girls here. The Aubrey girl and her friend, sir."

"Here? Girls?" Mr Smith looked at the

girls in astonishment. Then he clapped himself on the forehead and leapt from his chair. "Is one of you Jack Aubrey's daughter?" If he had sounded angry before, it was nothing to this.

"But, sir," protested Binoculars Man. "These are boys."

"Anyone can get a haircut," snapped the other, glaring at Hannah and Lizzie. Then he pointed at Lizzie. "You."

Fearfully Lizzie nodded.

Mr Barbed Wire exploded. "You stupid little idiots!" he fumed. "How could you behave like this? Your parents have been out of their minds with worry." He stormed about the room. "You idiots – you thoughtless fools! How could you do it to them?" Hannah and Lizzie hung their heads.

He told them of their parents' horror on discovering Lizzie's trick with the letters, the shame poor Bella felt. He told them how the Aubreys had rushed back from Germany – "He said he couldn't possibly work until he found you –" and how anxiously they and

Ruth Wilder had waited by the phone for news.

"Only it never came..." For a moment, Mr Smith turned to Binoculars Man. "Tell the police what we've got – and get on to the Aubreys right away."

Ashamed as Lizzie felt, there was one other thing that bothered her. If only Mr Smith wasn't so angry... She took courage.

"Sir – please," she said wheezily. "Where's Vanilla Fudge? Our puppy?"

"Puppy?" Mr Smith growled. "Dead for all I know. Chasing sheep probably."

Hannah and Lizzie looked at him in horror. It was only too possible.

Then everything happened at once. The storm cloud that had been threatening, burst – and Lizzie started to have an asthma attack.

Mr Smith stopped raging. "Doesn't she have an inhaler?"

"She used it up ages ago," Hannah said. "She hasn't needed one up till now."

"I see." He looked at Lizzie. "Right." He

felt for the keys in his pocket. "Hospital for you, young lady. We mustn't lose any more time."

He scooped her up in his arms. "You do the doors," he snapped to Hannah. "Quickly now."

Lizzie was no lightweight. Face set with effort, Mr Smith carried her out. Every now and then he had to put her down to rest. It wasn't far to the Range Rover but it seemed to take ages.

Lizzie was very bad. She was crying, talking about her parents, and about Vanilla Fudge. She was shivering now, and her lips had turned blue.

"Ssh, don't try to talk," Hannah said. But it was no good. Lizzie was too worried.

Mr Smith leapt into the car and they bumped along towards the gate. Hannah held Lizzie's hand and stroked it, talking quietly about anything she could think of – the suppers they had cooked, and mostly about Vanilla Fudge. "I'm sure she's all right," she said. But she didn't really think so.

Suddenly Mr Smith shouted. "Are you strapped in? Hold tight!" He screeched to a sudden halt and reversed a short way. "I thought I saw—"

Hannah looked up. She peered across the field to the barbed wire fence. Just behind it was a tall, thin man with a dog on a lead.

Hannah gasped. "Lizzie! She's all right! It's Vanilla Fudge." But Lizzie's eyes were dull. It was clear she didn't believe Hannah.

Yelling to Mr Smith to wait, Hannah jumped from the car. She cupped her hands and called. "Vanilla Fudge! Here girl!"

Seeing what was wanted, the thin man un-clipped her lead. They weren't far from the oak tree the girls had climbed in by. Vanilla Fudge raced along the fence, dived into the fox hole and was heading towards them at an ear-flapping gallop.

"So that's how she got in," muttered Mr Smith. "Hey!" For Vanilla Fudge had scrambled into the car and was covering the beautiful leather seats with muddy pawprints. "Hhmph!" he said crossly to Hannah. "Now your friend's seen the dog you'd better keep it off: it won't help the asthma to have a dog leaping all over her. I suppose it'd better spoil my front seat too." So for the whole journey, Vanilla Fudge sat on the front seat, delightedly breathing doggy breath all over Mr Smith, who didn't like it one bit.

Lizzie still looked blue, but she had stopped crying and seemed less frightened.

Mr Smith was a good driver – safe but fast. As they sped along he looked in his mirror at the two girls behind him. "What do they say in the village? About me, I mean."

Hannah didn't know what to answer; what she had heard was mostly rather rude. "Er – antiques," she said at last.

Mr Smith laughed out loud. "I don't believe that for a moment," he said. "What is it? Madness? Gun-smuggling?"

Hannah hesitated. "Well, he does have a gun – your man with binoculars."

"Ah, Simon – yes, he does – but it's not the kind of gun that kills people – or dogs very easily. It's for the birds."

"Killing birds?" Hannah was mystified.

"No, no, no!" Mr Smith laughed. "Quite the opposite: protecting them. I own a large chain of electrical shops – very dull. Birds are my real passion. That's what all the barbed wire is about. You see, my little valley is a place where a very rare species of hawk nests – the Red Kite."

"Oh!" said Hannah. Suddenly everything began to make sense – the hawks, the pictures on the walls.

"That's why I bought it. The bell tower makes a perfect hide. And Jack Aubrey's sorting me out a new computer system so I won't have to go away so much. I'll be able to work there and keep an eye on the birds at the same time. They are so rare, they need protection at all times – that's what Simon's for."

"And the gun?"

"Just to frighten people off. People are the greatest menace." He winked into the mirror. "Like the two egg thieves I so unkindly locked up."

"Egg thieves?" Hannah said. "You thought we were egg thieves?"

"I had good reason: Red Kites very nearly died out completely in Britain because of them." He began to get angry at the very thought. "They make my blood boil. I've got six pairs this year – that's out of only fifty in the country. Thanks to the Nature Conservancy Council they are beginning to increase nicely. But last year the NCC had terrible trouble with egg collectors. It takes twelve people to keep a twenty-four hour watch. With the barbed wire, I can manage with just Simon and me."

Mr Smith coughed. "Er – maybe I was a bit hasty. I'm sorry. It's just that I get so fond of my birds, I can't bear it when people want to hurt them in any way."

Just then they turned in through the hospital gates. Two nurses were waiting with a wheelchair for Lizzie. They whisked her off. One of them said to Hannah, "You come in too. There's someone waiting for you."

"Hhmph!" said Mr Smith to Vanilla

Fudge. "And I get lumbered with you."
Vanilla Fudge flopped into his lap and
breathed heavily, horribly, in his face.

Chapter 23

"Mum!" Hannah couldn't believe her eyes.

"I'll tell you off later," Ruth Wilder said. "Just now all I want is a big, big hug."

"Me too," said Hannah, and burst into tears.

When they had both recovered a bit, Ruth Wilder said, "Mr and Mrs Aubrey are here too. They're in with Lizzie."

"How did the police find us?" Hannah asked. "How did they know where we were?"

Ruth Wilder smiled. "When Vanilla Fudge slipped out through the badger hole, you were shut up again, weren't you? Anyway, the men scared her. So she went straight back to the place she knew – Uncle Ralph's cottage."

"And Uncle Ralph was there."

"Yes. He'd arrived the night before, and found your mysterious note and—"

"And no food," said Hannah hanging her head.

"No food, no wood, no gas, and a chewed up hearth-rug. He still didn't put two and two together until Vanilla Fudge trotted in through the door as if she owned the place, and demanded to be fed. He knew about you two disappearing, and about the puppy. He was on to us – and the police – at once."

"But how did you know we were at Mr Barbed Wire's?"

"Well, nobody thought of it at all. It was Vanilla Fudge again. When she saw Uncle Ralph hadn't got any food for her, she gave him a filthy look, and headed back to you. The police just followed."

It was a few days later at Uncle Ralph's cottage. Propped up in bed and surrounded by visitors, Lizzie was feeling much better. But she was very anxious, seeing them all together. She knew they had been discussing something between them. She also knew, sadly, that her mother couldn't live in the same house as Vanilla Fudge: it just wasn't fair to ask her to.

And this was where Mr Aubrey began. "I'm terribly sorry, Lizzie – "

"It's all right, Mum," Lizzie said. "I know how awful it feels to be allergic to things." She would give Vanilla Fudge to Hannah. It wouldn't be the same as owning her, but she could go and visit.

Mrs Aubrey smiled. "Thanks, darling – but listen to your father."

"Well," carried on Mr Aubrey. "As I say, I'm sorry that we can't have Vanilla Fudge at home but we've had another idea."

Lizzie settled back to listen.

"It involves me too," Ruth Wilder said. "And Hannah." Hannah wondered what could be coming.

"Hannah knows I've been looking for a new

job. Well, one has come up, at a boarding school not far from here."

"Here, in the country?" Hannah said.

"That's right." Ruth Wilder smiled. "I've been speaking to the headmaster, and he'd very much like to give me the job. He's offered you a place at the school, Hannah, on an Art Scholarship." Seeing Hannah's puzzled face, she laughed.

"I got him to ring Mrs Currey. She told him how well you'd done in the competition. She also faxed him some of your Vanilla Fudge drawings. He was very impressed."

Lizzie tried to say "That's marvellous Hannah," but the words stuck in her throat. She felt wretched: she would lose both Vanilla Fudge and Hannah – the first real friend she had had – all in one go.

It was Mrs Aubrey who noticed her first. She reached out and took her daughter's hand. "Lizzie. There is a solution. I know you've had an attack, but that was caused by the terrible stress you were under. In fact, you look a completely different child to a few weeks ago – all this fresh air and walking has done great good." Mrs Aubrey paused, and looked to see how Lizzie would take it.

"Would you like to go to the same school – as a boarder? As you've been ill, you wouldn't live with the other boarders. Instead, you'd live somewhere nearby with Hannah and her mother."

Just then there was a scrabbling at the door.

" – and Vanilla Fudge," said Mr Aubrey. "We'll miss you dreadfully, Lizzie – but Ralph says we can use the cottage nearly every weekend. You'll be able to come and stay with us here."

Lizzie looked at Hannah uncertainly. "Don't you mind me coming to live with you?"

"Mind?" said Hannah. "Why should I mind?" She grinned. "After all, now you know all the important things in life – making your bed, cooking spaghetti bolognese."

Lizzie flushed with pleasure.

The scrabbling at the door became frantic. This time it was accompanied by a high-pitched whine of deepest misery.

"I'll see to her," Hannah said, getting up.

Lizzie called her back. "Tell her," she said, "Tell her I'll come soon, and tell her that this time – for sure – it'll be for always and always."

HIPPO ANIMAL STORIES

*If you like animals, then you'll love
Hippo Animal Stories!*

Look out for:

Animal Rescue by Bette Paul

Tessa finds life in the country *so* different from life in
the town. Will she ever be accepted? But everything
changes when she meets Nora and Ned who run the
village animal sanctuary, and becomes involved in a
struggle to save the badgers of Delves Wood
from destruction . . .

Thunderfoot by Deborah van der Beek

Mel Whitby has always loved horses, and when she
comes across an enormous by neglected horse in a
railway field, she desperately wants to take care of it.
But little does she know that taking care of
Thunderfoot will change her life forever . . .

A Foxcub Named Freedom
by Brenda Jobling

A vixen lies seriously injured in the undergrowth. Her
young son comes to her for comfort and warmth. The
cub wants to help his mother to safety, but it is
impossible. The vixen, sensing danger, nudges him
away, caring nothing for herself – only for
his freedom . . .

Hippo Fantasy

Lose yourself in a whole new world, a world where anything is possible – from wizards and dragons, to time travel and new civilizations . . . Gripping, thrilling, scary and funny by turns, these Hippo Fantasy titles will hold you captivated to the very last page.

The Night of Wishes
Michael Ende (author of *The Neverending Story*)

Malcolm and the Cloud-Stealer
Douglas Hill

The Wednesday Wizard
Sherryl Jordan

Ratspell
Paddy Mounter

Rowan of Rin
Emily Rodda

The Practical Princess
Jay Williams

Robert Swindells

**"Faithful, fearless, full of fun,
Winter, summer, rain or sun,
One for five, and five for one –
THE OUTFIT!"**

*Meet The Outfit – Jillo, Titch, Mickey and Shaz. Share in
their adventures as they fearlessly investigate any mystery,
and injustice, that comes their way . . .*

Move over, Famous Five, The Outfit are here!

The Secret of Weeping Wood

The Outfit are determined to discover the truth about the
eerie crying, coming from scary Weeping Wood. Is the
wood really haunted?

We Didn't Mean To, Honest!

The marriage of creepy Kenneth Kilchaffinch to snooty
Prunella could mean that Froglet Pond, and all its
wildlife, will be destroyed. So it's up to The Outfit to
make sure the marriage is off . . . But how?

Kidnap at Denton Farm

Farmer Denton's new wind turbine causes a protest
meeting in Lenton, and The Outfit find themselves in
the thick of it. But a *kidnap* is something they didn't
bargain for . . .

The Ghosts of Givenham Keep

What is going on at spooky Givenham Keep? It can't be
haunted, can it? The Outfit are just about to find out . . .